THE
DEVIL'S
CONCUBINE

By

Jaide Fox

Fantasy Romance

New Concepts   Georgia

Be sure to check out our website for the very best in fiction at fantastic prices!

When you visit our webpage, you can:
* Read excerpts of currently available books
* View cover art of upcoming books and current releases
* Find out more about the talented artists who capture the magic of the writer's imagination on the covers
* Order books from our backlist
* Find out the latest NCP and author news--including any upcoming book signings by your favorite NCP author
* Read author bios and reviews of our books
* Get NCP submission guidelines
* And so much more!

We offer a 20% discount on all new Trade Paperback releases ordered from our website!

Be sure to visit our webpage to find the best deals in e-books and paperbacks! To find out about our new releases as soon as they are available, please be sure to sign up for our newsletter (http://www.newconceptspublishing.com/newsletter.htm) or join our reader group (http://groups.yahoo.com/group/new_concepts_pub/join)!

The newsletter is available by double opt in only and our customer information is *never* shared!

Visit our webpage at:
www.newconceptspublishing.com

The Devil's Concubine is an original publication of NCP. This work has never before appeared in book form. This work is a novel. Any similarity to actual persons or events is purely coincidental.

New Concepts Publishing, Inc.
5202 Humphreys Rd.
Lake Park, GA 31636

ISBN 1-58608-776-2
February 2006 © Jaide Fox
Cover art (c) copyright 2006 Eliza Black

NCP books are available at special quantity discounts for bulk purchases for sales promotions, premiums, fund raising, or educational use. For details, write, email, or phone New Concepts Publishing, Inc., 5202 Humphreys Rd., Lake Park, GA 31636; Ph. 229-257-0367, Fax 229-219-1097; orders@newconceptspublishing.com.

First NCP Trade Paperback Printing: March 2006

Jaide Fox

OTHER TRADE PAPERBACKS FROM NEW
CONCEPTS PUBLISHING BY JAIDE FOX:

SKY PIRATES

ORGASMIZER9000 and other stories

THE FALLEN

TRIPPING THROUGH THE UNIVERSE

CAPTURED

ULTIMATE WARRIORS

INTERGALACTIC BAD BOYS: Book One and Two

WINTER THAW/HIS WICKED WAYS

THE SHADOWMERE TRILOGY

Chapter One

Talin's keen gaze was captured by a flutter of movement on the roof of King Andor's palace as he guided his mount through the castle gates and into the inner courtyard. The brightly colored veil of a maiden flashed again as he looked up and he saw a cluster of young women along the waist high walls that topped one wing of the palace. They returned his perusal with unabashed interest and his lips curled faintly, for he knew, being mere man children, they could not see him nearly as well as he could see them and no doubt thought subtlety was unnecessary.

A nervous flutter of feminine giggles tickled at his ears as one turned to look at someone beyond his view. "Princess Aliya! You must come to see!"

His interest instantly sharpened. Tilting his head, he listened for a response, frowning when he heard nothing and wondering if she'd only spoken so softly he'd failed to hear, or not at all.

No matter. The maid had spoken to her, the one he'd come so far to see, the great beauty the man children were crowing about and gathering to squabble over. He knew exactly where she was and it would be no great feat to join her there.

He'd intended to confront King Andor about the insult to the people of Goldone head on, but upon consideration he decided he was more interested in assuaging his curiosity about the Princess Aliya.

After studying the façade of the palace for several moments, he handed off the reins of his mount absently to a stable hand and casually strolled away from the crowd that had bottle necked at the main entrance to the castle. The crowd thinned as he walked, peared to a handful and then only the occasional passerby. Moving to a small outbuilding, he leaned back against the wall, folding his arms across his chest and pretending no more than a mild interest in the wall before him as he assessed it. When no one passed after several moments, he discarded his boots and peeled his breeches off, tossing them aside.

He was on the point of shifting fully when it occurred to him that doing so might make climbing through the narrow window above him a little difficult. Shrugging, he merely focused on morphing wings and talons for gripping and launched himself skyward. The climb was harder than he'd expected, for he'd moved into a narrow cul-de-sac and there was little in the way of air currents to aid him.

He was only slightly winded when he grasped the window ledge with his sharp talons, however. Morphing from wings to arms once more, he grasped the edges of the window and leapt down onto the stone floor of a corridor.

There were two guards standing stiffly erect outside a set of doors some ten feet from where he'd landed. Either he'd made more noise that he'd thought, or the movement caught the eye of one of the guards, for he turned his head curiously. Unhooking the whip coiled at his waist, Talin flicked. The leather snaked out, the tip curling tightly around the man's throat. Gasping, his eyes widening, he caught at the leather around his throat instinctively even as Talin yanked on the whip, jerking the man face down on the tiles.

Leaping forward and upward at almost the same instant, he caught the second guard with his talons around the throat, choking off a half uttered cry of alarm. His momentum slammed the guard backward into the wall. Talin released the man as he began to slide to the floor.

After staring down at his prey for several moments, he grabbed the man's armor and slugged him in the face with his fist. The guard's eyes rolled back in his head and, satisfied, Talon turned to the first. That one, he saw, was already turning blue in the face. Shrugging, he balled up his fist and knocked that guard out, as well.

Retrieving his whip, he glanced up and down the corridor and finally opened the door and peered inside. Finding the room empty, he morphed into full man once more, grabbed a man in each hand and dragged them inside. One was already beginning to come around. A quick search of a chest nearby turned up a marvelous collection of scarves. Using those, he bound and gagged both men, then strode across the room, checking at each window for guards.

There were two more guards on the roofs overlooking what he now saw was a garden of some sort, for potted trees and flowers grew there in profusion. It took a little longer than he liked to dispatch the last two guards because he was forced to climb the walls to get to them. Finally, however, he had neatly disposed of the possibility of interruption and merely vaulted over the low wall of the last post, landing lightly on the garden tiles.

* * * *

Emerging briefly from her own thoughts, Princess Aliya smiled absently at the maid who'd spoken to her. It seemed to be the response the maid had expected. She flitted away again, leaving Aliya to her thoughts once more.

The roof top garden was not a place for meditation at any time that her ladies were present. Today it was even less peaceful than usual. The maids flitted from one spot along the low wall that protected the outer edge of the garden to another, looking, and sounding, like a small flock of excited birds as they watched the activity below them, exchanging observations about the dignitaries arriving for the tournament.

Wryly, Princess Aliya thought that, from their behavior, one might almost believe one, or all, of them were watching the arrival of their own suitor.

She almost wished that were the case, but she wasn't entirely sure of why she wished it.

Almost two years to the day before, when preparations had been underway for her sixteenth birthday celebration, she had been as excited as any of her ladies were, certain that her father meant to settle her and that she would soon be overseeing her own household. She had been tremendously disappointed when that was not the case. She had reached marriageable age the year before and had not been settled, but she had been brought up to understand that her marriage would be of political significance. As disappointed and impatient for life as she was, she'd understood that her father needed time to weigh his decision carefully when there had been no less than three princes who had offered for her. She also understood that the decision was made even more difficult by the fact that others offered for her in the time that her father, King Andor, pondered his decision--powerful men that he had no wish to offend. She'd convinced herself that the celebration planned for her sixteenth birthday was also to be the occasion when she would at last be told who had been chosen for her. Again, she had been disappointed and so it had gone since. Each time her father had considered her suitors and concluded which would be best to choose to protect the interests of his kingdom and his daughter, a new suitor would appear upon their doorstep and he would go back to examining the situation.

She'd begun to think she would never be wed, or if she was that she would be long in the tooth and perhaps too old to bear children.

She had enjoyed the courtships. With each new suitor, she had found something to admire about him, something to appeal to the woman in herself, the mother, the princess and, occasionally, all three. It had not always been an easy task. Some had been young, barely old enough to be considered men at all, others more 'seasoned,' and still others quite old. Few of them were actually handsome, but they were quite presentable and only a couple had been completely unappealing physically.

Her opinion mattered to her father, but she was a woman full grown now, and she realized that her personal feelings could not be allowed to get in the way of a sound political decision so she preferred to keep those to herself.

In truth, she didn't feel more particularly drawn to one above another.

She supposed she wasn't as excited as her ladies because she had been disappointed so many times before and, although her father had announced that she would be bestowed upon the winner of the tournament, that he would allow 'right of might' to determine her fate, she didn't entirely believe that would settle the matter when she had girded herself so many times before and been disappointed.

After a time, she realized there was a niggling of disenchantment at the heart of her strange moodiness. As unnerving as it had been to imagine men fighting over the honor of her hand, it had also been exciting. There had been a sense that fate would choose the perfect man for her, that she could not make the wrong choice, or her father. She would be wed to the strongest and bravest warrior among them.

Politics had again intervened. The oldest and the youngest and least experienced of her suitors had complained that that was not a fair way to conclude the matter and they had been allowed to send their champions to fight in their place.

Now she might well end up with a man who was not strong and brave at all, but rather the man who'd paid the best warrior. And, regardless of her sensitivity to the issues at stake, she hardly felt that that was fair to her. She might end up with a grandfather ... or a boy!

That had always been a possibility, of course, because the young and virile did not always inherit a powerful kingdom, but it was very disappointing to be allowed to think she would have a skilled, fearless warrior as husband and then discover that might not be the case at all.

Sighing, she decided to try to put those anxieties from her mind. Now was not the time to be moping. There was to be feasting and entertainment of all sorts.

The tournament would be far more exciting than it had ever been before for the simple reason that she would wed whoever emerged as the best.

By her next birthday, she might well have a babe in her arms to cuddle!

That was almost as frightening a thought as it was thrilling, though, and she rose abruptly from the lounging couch where she'd been perched almost from the time she had come up to the gardens with her ladies.

Her beautiful gown, commissioned by her father especially for the occasion, was creased she saw in consternation when she looked down to smooth it. She was not generally prone to be so careless with her dress. Particularly not those things she owned that were as lovely as this gown, which had been fashioned of the finest silk and brocaded all over the bodice, the long, fitted sleeves, and the bell shaped skirt, and then sewn with seed pearls and tiny diamonds in a cunning floral design. From the moment she had had her first fitting, it had been her favorite, for the pale color seemed to her the perfect foil for her dark skin and the style was both fashionable and very flattering to her figure.

Sighing with irritation at herself for crimping it, she finally dismissed it and crossed the garden to join her ladies at the garden wall.

Leesa, the daughter of one of her father's highest advisors, turned at her approach. Her face crinkled with barely suppressed merriment. "I thought you would not be able to resist long!"

Aliya chuckled. "It is almost as frightening to watch as it is exciting," she confessed, keeping her voice low so that the others wouldn't hear her.

Several different emotions flickered across Leesa's face. "You are soon to be a bride. You should have no other thought in your head but the thrill of having so many magnificent warriors vying for your hand!"

Aliya smiled but shook her head. "It is here--I think," she said, kneading the coil of tension in her ribs. "But...." She broke off, staring down at the mass of humanity and carts and animals below. "It is a little overwhelming, too, don't you think?"

"I would be absolutely petrified if all of this were on my account," Leesa responded with a chuckle. "But you are Princess Aliya! The most beautiful princess in all the known world. You should be accustomed to this sort of-- adoration!"

Aliya's lips flattened. A faint frown drew her brows together. "That part is almost as scary as the rest, if you must know," she muttered. "It would almost be easier to think they had only come because they were so anxious to ally themselves to my father. It would not matter then if I was hump backed or lame--no one would be expecting perfection. What if ... what if the one chosen for me does not find me the least appealing as a woman? I had expected a wedding of political significance from the time I was a small child, but I am a woman now. I may have been born a princess, but I am still a woman and I want the same things that every woman wants; a husband whom I can love and respect that will care for me."

Leesa stared at her in genuine confusion. "But ... you are beautiful!"

Aliya rolled her eyes. "I am a princess! Do you think I do not know that that is why I am considered beautiful? My father loves me. That is why he thinks I am beautiful. And everyone else--well they would not like to displease him, I am sure."

"Your grace, please forgive me if I am too familiar, but-- that is just plain silly! Have you not looked in your mirror?"

Aliya blushed but brushed aside Leesa's anxiety that she would offend her princess. "I am afraid if I look too hard I will see the imperfections I fear are there," she said wryly. "Anyway, I can not be an impartial judge and beyond that, beauty is what pleases the eye of those who look upon it. It can not be the same for everyone who looks. Even if I was enchanted with myself, it does not necessarily follow that anyone else would agree with me--if I was not a princess."

"But that is only a part of what disturbs you?" Leesa asked perceptively.

Aliya frowned. "I know what my duty is and I will not shirk my responsibilities."

"But?"

Aliya shrugged and laughed, but wryly. "I do hope that I will not find myself wed to some grandfather."

In an unaccustomed display of affection, Leesa slipped an arm around Aliya's waist and gave her a consoling squeeze. "Then you are right. You are not so different from the rest of us. You must try not to worry too much about such things. If he is very old, he will be less likely to trouble you in the marital bed, more likely to cherish you for yourself, and be considerate enough to leave you a young widow."

Aliya bit her lip to contain a smile. "That is not a very charitable sentiment," she said primly.

"Perhaps not, but it is very true, nevertheless, and I see you are feeling much more yourself already. Now, stroll with me. I saw a particularly handsome young warrior arrive at the gate only a few moments ago and I am sure he must be in the bailey by now so that we can view him much better."

A chuckle escaped Aliya. "How do you know that he is handsome? You could not possibly have seen him well enough from here to tell if he was well favored or not!"

"Deduction, dear princess!" Leesa replied promptly. "I could see quite well enough to discern that his hair was a glorious shade of gold, and his figure a very fine one. For the rest, I am assured by the way all the ladies he passed who stopped to gape at him that he is extraordinarily well favored."

Aliya gurgled with laughter. "Perhaps they only stopped to gawk because he was quite hideous?"

Leesa grinned but shook her head. "If that were the case then they would have fled, not stopped to stare."

Intrigued, Aliya allowed Lady Leesa to lead her to the other end of the garden. To her disappointment, but without much surprise, she saw no one fitting the 'golden young god' Leesa had described. "You were only teasing me," she said accusingly as she turned from her perusal of the guests gathered below them.

Leesa was frowning. "Truly, I was not. Look there. He was mounted upon that great golden horse there with the trappings of red and black."

A thud not far behind them distracted them both. As Aliya turned, she was stunned to discover a strange man had just landed in the garden, having apparently leapt down from the roof just above it, or perhaps from the window of the room overlooking the rooftop garden, though how he could have accessed either with the palace guards everywhere was a mystery to her.

As he strode purposely toward her, she glanced around instinctively to look for the guards. A needle of alarm stabbed through her when she saw the two who'd been standing near the garden entrance were nowhere in sight. By the time she'd checked every post and found every man missing she was beginning to feel downright faint with fear. "The guards are gone," she whispered a little breathlessly, transferring her gaze to the man approaching them.

Striding purposefully, he had already covered more than half the distance that had separated them when she had first seen him and yet she sensed no urgency in his movements, and certainly there was no stealth in his approach.

A flicker of doubt went through her. Did he present a danger or not?

He was not armed.

He was scarcely even decently dressed for she saw that not only were his feet bare, but he wore nothing more than a scanty breechcloth below the waist, leaving the entirety of his golden brown flesh from hip to foot exposed. The vest that covered his chest was little more than woven strips of leather, open along the sides from shoulder to waist, save for the woven bits of leather that held it together.

A coiled whip was secured at his waist.

A horse master from some distant, primitive kingdom?

Aliya dragged her gaze from him as her other ladies, apparently becoming aware of the stranger and the absence of the guards, scurried to her side--whether to protect her or to draw courage from her presence, she wasn't certain which.

When she returned her attention to the stranger, she saw that he had halted little more than a yard away and was surveying her and her ladies with interest.

A sensation midway between fear and fascination went through her. His features were harshly angular, almost predatory. For all that, he was the most striking man she had ever seen and she felt a sensation wash through her that made her feel weak and faint and breathless with excitement all at the same time.

The glint of precious metal caught her gaze as he moved closer still and she glanced at the rows of buttons that adorned the front of the vest he wore. Each bore a royal crest of some house she was unfamiliar with.

Was he one of the royals who'd gathered for the tournament, she wondered, feeling her heart flutter anxiously at the thought?

Dragging her gaze from the crest, she met his sharp gaze. His eyes, almost the same golden brown shade as his hair, raked over her and her ladies boldly.

"I have come for the princess, Aliya," he said finally.

Blinking in surprise, Aliya and her ladies exchanged questioning glances.

"I am Princes Aliya," Leesa said, stepping forward, her voice quavering ever so slightly. "What is it you want of me?"

Stunned, Aliya could only gape at her maid.

The stranger looked Leesa over critically and dismissed her, returning his attention to Aliya and her other ladies. Even as his gaze lit upon Aliya, her lady, Beatrice, stepped in front of her. "It is alright, Lady Leesa. I am Princess Aliya."

The stranger strode toward her without a word, grasped her shoulders and set her aside. His piercing gaze swept over Aliya. "I have come a very long way to see the woman that so many men are willing to die for."

Aliya swallowed with an effort, still too stunned by the stranger's brash behavior to sort her chaotic thoughts. "Who are you?" she whispered.

His hard, sharply etched lips curled faintly in something approximating a smile, but the amusement did not reach his eyes. "I am King Talin, hereditary ruler of the tribe of the Golden Falcon."

Chapter Two

Pinned by his hard gaze, Aliya suddenly found herself alone, for her ladies were under no such constraint. The moment he spoke, they uttered gasps and weak squeaks of fear and scurried to put some distance between themselves and the object of their terror.

"An unnatural," Leesa uttered in a breathless whisper.

Talin slid a speculative glance at the cringing ladies and then returned his attention to Aliya. Looking her over for all the world like a merchant, he surveyed her with interest from head to toe and then moved slowly around her with the same attitude of interest.

Enthralled as she had been from the moment she'd seen him clearly, and as frozen as she had been more by surprise than fear when she discovered he was an unnatural, a sense of outrage began to seep into Aliya at his proprietary attitude. She was a princess! Her father's heir! How dare the man behave as if she was some common harlot offering her wares!

And him trying to decide whether she was *worth* the price she'd demanded, which was almost more insulting than the latter!

Her eyes narrowed as he faced her once more.

"Leave at once and I won't summon my father's guards to cut you down like a dog!" she said tightly.

Surprise flickered over his features briefly. It was replaced almost at once with true amusement and Aliya discovered that even her anger wasn't proof against that smile, for her heart seemed to turn over in her chest as it transformed his harsh features. "I hail from the tribe of

Golden Falcon, not the wolf, but by all means summon them."

Moistening her lips, Aliya glanced around a little hopelessly for the guards she knew had already had been dispatched--by this man--she realized now. "How did you get up here?"

His amusement vanished. "The arrogance of your kind never ceases to amaze me--or infuriate me, for that matter. I am man beast--or, as your maid so rudely pointed out--an unnatural. Inaccurate and insulting, implying that only your kind is 'natural.' I am as nature made me, so I can not be an 'unnatural.' Moreover, if you'll forgive me for being equally rude, the many people who make up the kingdoms of the 'unnatural' are far superior in every way to your own kind. It is a mistake to think we are as limited in our abilities as you are. For my kind, there are always ways."

Aliya couldn't help the blush that darkened her skin and could only be glad that she was not as light skinned as the man standing before her. For the pale skinned, their discomfiture was always blatantly apparent to all. "Why are you here?"

His lips thinned. "Because I was not invited."

A frown creased Aliya's brow. "I don't understand."

"You comprehend insult, though, don't you?"

The blush that had barely receded flooded back with such a vengeance that it made her feel hot all over. She moistened her lips. "There was no intent to offer insult."

He studied her thoughtfully. "And yet I am. I wonder why? I hadn't thought that I was so thin skinned as to see insult where there was none."

"My apologies," Aliya said stiffly. "My father only thought to settle a ... uh ... dispute between our kingdom and those invited here today."

"Which includes every kingdom in the known world, save those of the--ah--'unnaturals.' But you apologize so prettily for the unintended insult that I have to wonder if perhaps my invitation went astray? Am I to understand that I have been laboring under an insult that was purely accidental? If so, then tell me now and I will summon the heirs to the other kingdoms of the many peoples of the man beast so that they, too, can vie for the honor of allying themselves to your father and winning the hand of such a lovely maiden."

Aliya stared at him in dismay. Unfortunately, he was right. Her father had very deliberately excluded those of the kingdoms of the unnatural. She had certainly not argued the decision--not that she did in general--but she was no keener on the notion of being wed to an unnatural than her father was.

His brows rose when she remained silent. "You deeply regret, but...?"

As skilled as she had thought she was in diplomacy, Aliya could think of nothing at all to say. He'd very effectively boxed her into a corner. There was no way she could claim that the slight hadn't been intentional without also agreeing that everyone, without exception, was welcome to take part in the tournament.

The plain fact of the matter was that the unnaturals could draw upon powers the naturals couldn't and if they did take part, she was going to end up the bride of some 'man beast' as he seemed to prefer to call them.

If she stalled long enough, though, surely someone would discover the guards?

"This entire dispute has already grown way out of proportion," she hedged.

"I couldn't agree more," he retorted, his voice carrying an edge. "Even I find you quite lovely--for a royal--but not necessarily so rare a jewel as to warrant such a furor."

Aliya felt heat rise in her face again, felt a pang of hurt, too, that he'd pointed out she wasn't nearly as beautiful as everyone had proclaimed her to be, or at least that he didn't agree. "I never claimed to be," she said stiffly. "Nor my father for that matter. Most of these royals gathered here have never even set eyes on me. This isn't about me at all. They are only here because they want to ally themselves with my father."

"And yet," he said thoughtfully, "I spied at least four who'd crossed the sea, and I have to wonder what possible advantage they might find in allying themselves with a kingdom so far from their borders? I must have missed something rather important, because I've seen nothing particularly valuable in your father's kingdom--beyond the daughter he dotes upon, and as I already pointed out, that is a matter of opinion."

Distress filled her. With an effort, she tamped it. It wasn't as if she actually cared what he thought of her, after all. "Now that you've come all this way to fling insults in my face are you quite satisfied?"

"Not hardly," he growled, surging closer abruptly so that his face loomed in her vision and his warm breath caressed her cheeks. "I confess I had something more murderous in mind for the insult to me and my people, but now that I am here it occurs to me that there is restitution that you can offer that might appease my sense of injury."

Aliya swallowed with an effort. "What sort of restitution? My father will pay--"

"Indeed he will--with his greatest treasure."

Aliya's jaw dropped. "Marry you, you mean?" she gasped in both surprise and outrage at his audacity.

He laughed, but the sound had no humor to it. "I would not sully my line, or insult my people by producing inferior offspring to rule behind me. If you please me, I might consider taking you as my concubine."

Shock went through Aliya. Before thaw could set in, she heard a shout behind her. "Run, Princess!"

She stumbled when she was shoved aside, still too stunned for many moments to figure out what was happening. As another of her ladies, Maude, the youngest, grabbed her hand and tugged on it, however, she followed the pull in blind instinct, lifting the heavily brocaded skirt of her gown to keep from tripping as she burst into a clumsy run.

She had not gotten far when something hot snaked around her waist and tightened, yanking her to a stop and jerking her hand from Maude's. She barely had time to register the fact that some sort of cord had encircled her waist when another hard yank sent her flying backwards. She struggled to get her feet beneath her.

She didn't succeed. Instead, she sprawled on her backside. When she looked up in stunned surprise, she discovered she now lay in the shadow of an enormous bird of prey.

Frightened as she was, she realized that as he'd shifted, he'd dropped the whip he'd used to lasso her and drag her back.

Uttering a sharp gasp, Aliya rolled over and began to crawl quickly away again. Her progress was impeded by her maids, who had banded together to try to defend her, closing in on the man beast and battering at him with their fists since they had no weapons. Pride and shame collided inside of her--that her ladies were brave enough, and loved her well enough, to risk their lives trying to protect her-- and shame that she could do nothing but try to crawl away like a coward.

She was more of a danger to them if she stayed than if she escaped, though, because they would continue the struggle as long as she was there and needed protection.

Despite their efforts, she made little headway. She'd barely managed to clear the shifting, struggling group when she heard a chorus of screams as he flung them from his path. A split second later, something huge and thick curled around her waist.

Aliya screamed when she looked down and discovered great talons biting tightly into her flesh, so tightly she could scarcely draw a breath. She managed to scream, though, when a tremendous gust of air pelted her and she felt herself rising free of the garden floor.

For many moments, she fought mindlessly against the grip around her, so intent on breaking free that it was several moments before she actually took in her surroundings. When she did, the darkness of sheer terror washed over her for her ladies had shrunk below her until they appeared to be little more than insects, and then quickly became mere dots of color. The sense that she was suffocating clawed at her mind, bringing her focus to one thing only, the need to breathe. It was the last thing she remembered before her entire world went black.

Discomfort roused her some time later. Disoriented, it took Aliya several moments to figure out why she was so uncomfortable. A jolt of fear driven adrenaline went through her when she remembered, and her eyes popped open. The moment her eyes focused another shaft of alarm went through her for she could see little beyond the white, misty clouds that surrounded her.

She didn't know if she was glad or sorry that she couldn't. So long as she couldn't actually see the ground far below her, she could comfort herself with the thought that she might not be as high as it seemed.

But then again, there were the clouds.

Almost upon the thought, they began to thin. Her stomach, even cramped as it was by the grip around her waist and her own free hanging weight, seemed to lift and then fall again. Pressure built in her ears and then dissipated with a startling pop as she swallowed against the knot of fear in her throat that felt like her heart.

Dark jagged rocks seemed to reach up toward her from below, further terrorizing her as it occurred to her to wonder if he'd only brought her to this place to dash her body upon them.

How far had they come, she wondered?

She had never been beyond the borders of her father's kingdom, and she could not ever recall having seen the like of this, even in the distance.

Her fear subsided slightly as she searched her mind for an answer. Was this the land of the unnaturals, she wondered? Or was it further still?

The answer seemed to appear before her almost as if her questions had conjured it. One strangely shaped peak, rising almost like a spire into the sky supported a 'platter' of rock. Atop that slab of stone more stone rose, but these had not been formed haphazardly by nature. A castle, starkly beautiful with its tall, graceful towers, and carved of the same stone, had been built upon the seemingly precarious perch.

Aliya knew immediately that she was gazing upon the castle of King Talin.

She was lost, she realized in dismay. Even if her maids had managed to raise the alarm, there was no way any normal human could ever reach this place among the clouds.

The thought led her abruptly back to the battle in her garden. Had he slain ladies as well as her guards?

A different sort of horror filled her as that thought materialized in her mind. After struggling to sort through the disjointed images in her memory, though, she was relieved that she could remember the expressions of dismay on her ladies' upturned faces as she'd been whisked away. He'd merely shoved them out of his way, she realized, remembering no sign of injury either on their persons or in their expressions.

A new anxiety rose, mixed liberally with hope and relief. Her ladies would tell her father what had happened. Somehow, he would find a way to rescue her. He would bring his army to destroy the kingdom of the Golden Falcons.

King Talin had started a war.

Chapter Three

As they drew nearer the dark castle of King Talin, Aliya noticed strange protrusions along each tower. They were very like balconies, except that there was no low wall or balustrade to protect the unwary from a deadly misstep. The man beast approached one such protrusion, hovering just above it. Before Aliya had quite grasped why he was doing so, the great bird's talons abruptly released her. Instinctively, she sucked in a sharp gasp as she felt herself falling. The drop was no more than two or three feet, but she was numb from cold and restricted circulation. Her knees buckled the moment her feet met the solid surface. She uttered a cry, her arms pin wheeling as she tried to catch her balance and failed, sprawling precariously near the edge. She froze when she stopped, unable to command herself to move at all as she stared down at the abyss below her. A thud close by jolted through her abject terror and she jerked her head in the direction of the sound.

King Talin had landed at the very rim of the perch she laid upon, morphing into the form of a man once more even as he set his feet upon the ledge.

The distraction was sufficient to unfreeze her limbs and, in a blind panic to put some distance between herself and the drop-off, Aliya scrambled crab like away from the terrifying edge. Her shoulder made impact against stone so abruptly it sent stinging pain all the way through her, but she realized it was the edge of an opening and rolled onto her belly, racing away as quickly as she could on her hands and knees. She didn't stop until she met another wall on the opposite side of the sprawling tower room from the gaping mouth and tongue of stone. Even with the added distance, her chest still felt so constricted with fear that she could hardly drag in a decent breath of air. The muscles in her jaws cramped, trembling until her teeth were rattling together.

A dark form filled the arched doorway, capturing her attention. Talin, she saw, had followed her. His expression was a mixture of anger and confusion as he met her round eyed gaze.

Shuddering, Aliya glanced past him at the view beyond the doorway for a moment before she returned her attention to her captor. As long as she didn't look directly at the yawning space beyond the doorway, she felt marginally safe, could feel some of the blind panic begin to recede.

Talin tilted his head at her curiously. "You have never seen a man beast before?"

There was a questioning lilt to the statement, but she realized it *was* a statement and required no response, which was just as well since her vocal chords seemed as frozen as everything else.

"Your fear is … excessive. I will not harm you."

Aliya stared at him blankly, trying to wrap her mind around what he'd said.

He thought his beast form had frightened her out of her mind, she decided.

It had been unnerving to say the very least.

The view from the clouds was what had frightened her out of her wits, however, and the drop onto the open balcony. She had thought for several terrifying moments that she would roll off to fall endlessly until she crashed into the rocks below.

Another shudder went through her as her mind instantly conjured the image.

He wouldn't harm her? He'd made it very clear when he'd taken her that he meant to turn her into his whore. Exactly what constituted *harm* in his mind, she wondered a little wildly? Ruining her life wasn't harm enough?

Destroying all chance of happiness for her wasn't harm? Was she supposed to just take his word for it that he would not beat or torture her, merely rape her? Because he would have to force himself upon her. She would never yield to him willingly. "My father will come for me," she stammered abruptly, with something akin to childish bravado since she knew very well that there was no chance at all that her father could ever rescue her from this palace in the sky.

Talin crouched in front of her so that he was more or less eye level with her. When he did, she drew her knees up tightly against her chest. "He will not," he said grimly. "The sooner you accept that, the better."

A crushing sense of defeat washed over her at his calm pronouncement, because she knew he was right. She was completely at his mercy and she wasn't at all certain he had any. She could do nothing but accept--whatever he meant to do with her. Her mind simply refused to furnish her with any speculation as to what that might entail.

She surged to her feet, flattening herself against the wall at her back. "He would rather I was dead than dishonored, my belly swollen with the babe of a … a…!" she stammered a little hysterically, breaking off when she found she couldn't remember what he'd called his people.

His lips tightened, his eyes narrowing with anger as he, too, came slowly to his feet. "Such a loving father," he murmured.

"*I* would prefer it!" Aliya screamed at him with fury borne of fear. Pushing away from the wall abruptly, she raced toward the arch and the blue beyond. *Don't think about it!* She commanded herself. *For your honor, and your father's honor, just do it!*

She caught him by surprise. She'd already reached the archway and burst through it when something white hot snaked around her waist, yanking her to a halt on the very edge of the precipice and crushing the air from her lungs as if she'd been punched in the chest. For a handful of heartbeats she stared down at the clouds and rocks below her and then, as suddenly as a door slamming closed, blackness descended.

Her last thought as the darkness consumed her was relief. She was never going to know when she landed.

Talin uttered a curse when she began to crumple, jerking on the whip. The tug tumbled her backwards as she began to sink to the floor, keeping her from pitching forward and off of the balcony, but he saw immediately that she would be injured regardless. Uttering another curse, he surged toward her, catching her shoulders before she could crack her head on the stone floor.

Angry and shaken, he scooped her up from the floor jerkily and stalked across the tower room and out into the stairwell. She roused when he was halfway down, but apparently she was still too disoriented to entirely assimilate what had happened. He knew the moment full awareness finally hit her for she went from limp to stiff as a board.

He tightened his grip on her and negotiated the last of the stairs.

"I am perfectly capable of walking," she said tightly.

Still furious, he set her on her feet abruptly.

She wobbled, but managed to stiffen her spine and lock her knees as he gripped her upper arm and hauled her along the corridor that led to the great room.

"Reyhan!" he bellowed.

The soldier, who'd been in the process of taking a swig of ale, jerked, pouring a good portion down the front of his leather jerkin. Slamming the tankard on the trestle table before him, he surged to his feet abruptly, brushing at the dampness on his jerkin as he hurried to answer the summons.

"Sire!"

Talin shoved the woman toward his guard. "Take her into the dungeon and secure her," he growled. "Make sure she can not harm herself, else it'll cost you your hide."

Reyhan's eyes widened fractionally, but he grabbed the woman firmly by one arm. "Yes, Sire!"

Talin looked her over speculatively. "And watch yourself. I imagine she would just as soon slit your throat as not if she can get her hands on a blade."

Appalled and outraged, it took Aliya several moments to realize he really intended to have her thrown into the dungeon. "I am a princess!" she stammered finally. "I demand the rights of my station. You can not throw me in the dungeon like a common felon!"

"You are in no position to demand anything!" Talin growled. "Take her."

She struggled briefly, but she either saw the futility of it or she decided it wounded her dignity to continue. She desisted after a moment, walking stiffly.

Talin watched the pair until Reyhan had vanished with her down the narrow corridor that led to the dungeon. Turning abruptly, he strode across the great hall, mounted the dais, and flung himself into his throne, drumming the fingers of one hand irritably on one chair arm. A round dozen men at arms were congregated in the great hall. He saw that they were gaping at him in stunned surprise and bent a furious glare upon them, whereupon they returned their attention to the games of chance they'd been amusing themselves with.

Scanning the hall, his gaze lit finally on the captain of the guard. "Solly!"

Solly jumped to his feet so quickly he nearly overturned the bench he'd been sitting on. Striding quickly across the hall, he went down on one knee before the dais. "Sire?"

"Round up a crew of carpenters. They are to install shutters and doors on every aperture--and bolts," Talin snarled. "Starting with the royal suite. I want my own suite finished by moon rise."

Solly gaped at him. "Sire?"

Talin's eyes narrowed. "Have you grown deaf?"

Shaking his head, Solly leapt to his feet. "No, Sire! I'll see to it, Sire."

When Solly had left, Talin sank into his own dark thoughts, drumming his fingers on the chair arm. The next time he glanced up it was to discover the last of his soldiers slinking quietly out the door.

He was tempted to summon them back and demand some sort of distraction, but decided after a moment that he preferred solitude in his current mood.

It had been a mistake to take her, but that realization angered him almost as much as the fact that he wasn't completely sure of why he had. He certainly had not gone to the Kingdom of Anduloosa for that purpose. In truth, he had had no clear idea of what he'd hoped to accomplish by going, other than to make it clear that he resented the insult to the man beasts in general and himself in particular.

Ordinarily, he was quite content that the inferior man children kept their petty little squabbles to themselves most of the time, rarely encroaching upon any of the kingdoms of the man beast. The tournament had been poor timing on their part, however. The clamoring of his beast to find a mate had become harder and harder to ignore in recent years, more difficult to ignore than the grumbling of his council that he had yet to take a queen and produce an heir to his throne.

Even so, he thought he could have ignored the uproar beyond the boundaries of his kingdom except for one minor fact--the princess, Aliya, was accounted the most beautiful and desirable of all, a pearl of such value that no kingdom in need of a queen wished to be excluded from the chance to claim her.

Until it had become known to him that kings and princess from far and wide were gathering to prove their worthiness of such a prize, he *had* ignored it. The fact that he had received no such invitation had begun to eat at him, however, long before he verified that not one royal from among the man beasts had been invited to take part in this great tournament.

He supposed he should have been appeased by that fact, not further enraged, but so it was. He had not been singled out for insult. He was not even important enough in their minds for that!

At first, he gave little thought to the princess herself, certain that their 'pearl' was likely as colorless and unappealing as the rest of her kind. Most likely he would have continued to believe that except for the growing numbers of men vying for her.

That gave him pause, despite his determination to regard her as unworthy of his time or interest. Could she really be so commonplace, he wondered, when so many were falling over themselves to fight for her? Or was it possible that she truly was a pearl beyond price?

And if so, then how dare they consider him unworthy without even allowing him to prove himself in battle?

When he had left his kingdom in his man form and disguised as a prince from another land, he had thought only to assuage his curiosity of the entire procedure and make it known to King Andor that he did not take such insults lightly and there would be a reckoning. For he'd fully intended to call his army to war and teach them the error of their ways if he was not completely satisfied when he left the kingdom of Anduloosa again.

He'd scarcely arrived, however, when he had caught a glimpse of the women in the rooftop garden and he'd decided in that moment to appease his curiosity about the princess herself. In doing so, he would put the fear of his wrath into King Andor by showing him just how vulnerable he and his family were.

All had gone well enough until he had found himself face to face with her. In truth, and though he hated to admit it even to himself, he scarcely recalled what had happened next. He had known the moment he set eyes upon her that the rumors were not exaggerations of a woman barely better than plain. She *was* beautiful, so flawlessly perfect in face and form that his beast had seized his rational mind, instantly demanding to claim her for his mate.

He did not regret it, although he well knew that his impulse would most likely spawn a war the likes of which no one had ever seen. In truth, he would have been quite willing to join the others who meant to prove their right to her in the contest of skills that had been set to take place.

If he had been thinking at all rationally, he would have gone at once to her father and demanded he retract the insult and allow him to take part, as well, to prove to her that he was a far more worthy warrior than all the others.

He had not been thinking rationally, though. He hadn't been able to think at all.

Grinding his teeth, he shifted in his throne and glared at the crew of carpenters that had begun to scurry back and forth through the hall, carrying tools and timbers. He was tempted to demand the lazy slugs use their gifts to move the materials instead of waddling clumsily along the ground, but it occurred to him that the task he'd set for them was easier performed in their man forms than bird and he tamped the urge.

Shoving himself from his chair abruptly, he stalked across the hall and opened the nearest window, pushing the crystal wide so that he could gaze out at the view beyond. Even the beauty and majesty of his domain failed to soothe him, however.

She had looked at him as if he was monster, so terrified she could barely move or speak.

He felt ill.

His impulsiveness had very likely cost him all he had sought to gain.

He should have wooed her as she deserved. He knew he was not nearly as handsome a man, as graceful, or as noble in bearing as when he took the form of a great, golden falcon, but he was certain he was not appallingly ugly. If he'd proven his strength and skill as a warrior, she would have admired that. She would have been pleased by the thought that her off spring would also be superior in every way--far superior to what she could have expected if she had been wed to some weakling man child!

Instead, she'd been so repulsed by the thought that she'd tried to fling herself off his balcony.

That angered him more than all the rest and he finally realized it did because it wounded him soul deep, that it was a blow to his ego he wouldn't easily recover from.

He felt even more ill when he recalled that he'd been so stunned by her sudden dash for freedom that it had taken him several moments to realize that she couldn't morph as he so easily did, that she had no wings to soar, that she would fall to her death.

And she knew it.

That was the hardest thing of all to swallow.

Scrubbing a hand over his face, he focused on the view once more and finally hopped onto the ledge and dove out, transforming himself as he dropped. Too restless to remain in his castle, he decided to go to the kingdom of Anduloosa and see what he'd unleashed.

Chapter Four

Talin discovered he didn't have to fly low over the castle of King Andor to see what he'd expected to see. Below him, the man children were dashing about frantically, like ants in a stirred anthill. Without difficulty, his keen sight easily picked out the purpose within the apparent pandemonium.

The man children were preparing for war.

And King Andor was not the only one readying for battle.

That was an unanticipated development.

He had given it little thought, but he supposed if he had he would have realized that the men who had traveled so far to vie for the fair maiden presently residing in his dungeon might not take their defeat well when they realized the prize had been snatched from their grasp.

Vaguely disconcerted, he saw that those households that had gathered for the tournament were now also preparing for war.

Still more in his beast mind than the more rational human side, he realized after a moment's consideration that he was more pleased by the results of his theft than disturbed. He had not left his lands intending to start a war between his kingdom and the kingdoms of the man children, but he did not feel a great deal of regret that he had succeeded in doing just that.

After a little further thought, he realized that he was actually grimly pleased that he had.

He would prove his right to the princess by might--not in a child's test of skills, in a tournament meant mostly for show, but on a true battlefield.

When he and his army had crushed the armies of the man children, Princess Aliya would see that he was far better suited to her as mate than any of the so called warriors that had gathered to claim her.

Satisfied with his observations, he caught an air current and drifted lower, low enough he caught the attention of those on the ground below him. When they began to shout excitedly and commenced to lobbing arrows and spears at him, he chuckled, adding insult to injury by dropping low enough he was almost within their range.

Resisting the temptation to drop lower still, and allow them a better target, just so he could demonstrate to them how impotent their efforts were, he caught an updraft and headed back to his own kingdom, Goldone.

It would be a month, at the very least, before they could move their clumsy army within reach of his own--for he had no intention of charging out to meet them like some green youth eager to fling himself upon a sword. He had time in plenty to plan his battle strategy and choose the place where they would meet and in the meanwhile, time to familiarize himself with his prize.

Perhaps he would woo her--just to please her. She seemed clever. No doubt it would not take her long to accept, but he wasn't certain he would be satisfied with mere acceptance. When he had first come upon her, she had looked at him with frank interest despite her uneasiness. Even with the lust boiling in his own veins, he was certain he hadn't imagined that.

The sun had dropped behind the mountains when he reached his palace once more. Lighting on the balcony of his own suite, he shifted, examining the stout door that now blocked the entrance critically. Satisfied that was sufficient to cage his little bird, he tried the latch.

He had to put his shoulder against the stout panel to push it open. Displeased by that, he was frowning when he finally stepped inside and turned to examine the hinges. "It scrapes the floor," he muttered to no one in particular.

Silence greeted that remark and he turned after a moment to study the carpenters, who'd frozen in place at his comment. The master carpenter hurried forward. "I will see to that myself, Sire. I will take it down at once and trim just a bit from the bottom and it will swing more easily."

Talin, finding he was in a far better mood than when he'd left the palace, merely nodded. "See to it that you do. The objective is to protect my beautiful princess--not suffocate your king. I am accustomed to air--and light." Dismissing the door, he strode about the suite, surveying the shutters that had been placed over the windows. "It will be as dark in here as the dungeon," he muttered irritably.

The master carpenter, who'd followed him, looked at the shutters in dismay. "Solly said you had ordered that shutters be placed over the windows. Did I misunderstand?"

"Shutters, yes--but there is no light. I have no view!"

"Bars, perhaps?" the carpenter suggested hesitantly. "They would allow a view and still protect the princess."

Talin frowned. "I like the idea of feeling caged even less." He thought it over. "And I do not care to make the princess feel a prisoner if it comes to that."

The carpenter gaped at him. "Uh--she is not a prisoner?"

Talin glared at him. "Certainly not! I have decided to keep her."

The carpenter's expression went perfectly blank. After a stunned moment, he remembered himself and studied his feet before the king could take exception to his obvious confusion over the distinction. "If I may suggest, Sire," he offered hesitantly, "with a little more time I am sure I could come up with a design for the shutters that will serve the purpose and still allow in light and view. I could do the same with the door, if you wish--cut some clever design into the panels?"

Talin considered it thoughtfully for several moments and finally nodded. "I will allow the princess to think of a design that pleases her. Women like to beautify their nests, do they not? It makes them feel--needed."

The carpenter frowned, feeling that the king had asked his opinion and wondering if he dared express it honestly. Finally, he merely shrugged. "I think it likely, Sire. She will certainly be more comfortable if she makes the place more like what she is familiar with."

Talin frowned, but thoughtfully. "An excellent suggestion!" he said finally, smiling broadly.

The carpenter blinked. "It was?" he asked, wondering what he'd suggested.

"I will send men to gather her cherished belongings and bring them here. Then she may arrange things just as she likes and she will be very pleased with my thoughtfulness."

The carpenter wasn't convinced. In his experience, once a man had thoroughly infuriated a woman by depriving her of her wishes--which he assumed King Talin had, for, from what he'd heard, the princess had been less than delighted to come--nothing short of bloodshed--his--would appease them, but he wisely kept that opinion to himself. Perhaps, he thought hopefully, she *would* be mollified at least a little that the king had put himself out to please her and it would stave off the battle of wills that was sure to erupt from the king's arrogance for a time.

There was going to be hell to pay, though, when King Talin discovered he would have to jump through hoops before she was completely satisfied that he'd been punished enough. He only hoped that he could complete his task and make himself scarce before all hell broke loose.

"We must wait upon that a little, though," King Talin continued after a few moments. "The man children are preparing for war. It will be difficult to retrieve her belongings before they have abandoned the castle."

The carpenter's brows rose. "The man children are warring?" he asked with interest.

"Aye."

"If I may be so bold as to ask, Sire, with whom?"

"Us," Talin said dismissively. "Finish up and move along. This will do for now. I must go to the dungeon and see if the princess has cooled her heels long enough to feel more reasonable."

Stunned as he was by the announcement that they were at war with the kingdom of Anduloosa, the last remark was enough to galvanize the master carpenter. "Cooled her heels?" he muttered when he was certain the king was out of earshot. It was all well and good that King Talin's temper seemed to have improved, but it wasn't likely to last once he reached the dungeon and discovered just how mistaken he was in his belief. "More likely she is thinking of ways to murder him in his bed."

Turning to his crew, he gauged their progress and decided they were close enough. "Make haste and finish. We do not want to be here when the king returns. I assure you, his mood will be foul, most foul!"

Chapter Five

The first thing Talin noticed as he descended the stairs into the dungeon was an ominous quiet. More accurately, he became aware that there was no noise, as he'd more than half expected, no curses, no wailing--not even so much as the scurrying of tiny rodent feet or the flutter of an insect. He did not, in fact, notice until he was halfway down that the silence was not the quiet of peace, but rather the pregnant pause before a storm of staggering magnitude.

Reaching the bottom, he held the torch high and glanced around.

No one was in sight and he frowned, wondering which cell Reyhan had placed the princess in. He glanced back up the way he had just come and then around the open area at the foot of the stairs. No one magically appeared to show him the way, but as he glanced down the narrow corridors leading off to the right, left and before him, he saw a flickering light at the end of the one on his right.

The interrogation room.

If that numbskull had taken her there, he decided angrily, he was going to take the hide off the fool!

Shoving the torch he'd carried down into a holder on the wall, he stalked down the narrow passage, coming to an abrupt stop at the other end as if he'd just struck an invisible wall.

He felt much as if he had, and that the concussion had not only knocked the wind out of him, but rattled his brain in his skull at the same time and scattered his wits.

Princess Aliya knelt on the opposite side of the room, her arms chained to posts on either side of her.

She was also the next thing to naked.

Like a sleep walker, he woke to find himself staring down at her, having no memory of crossing the room at all.

Saliva pooled in his mouth as he studied her stunning perfection, nearly strangling him when he recalled the need to swallow. He had thought from the moment he saw her that she was beyond compare, but he had not dreamed that the gown she wore hid as much of her lush beauty as it displayed. Her limbs were long and shapely, the skin seemingly as smooth and unblemished as fine silk, instantly conjuring an image in his mind of those arms and legs entwined about his body.

The imagery set his blood to a slow boil in his veins, pulsing in his skull and groin until he soon felt as if one, or both, would explode from the building pressure.

Her waist was tiny, curving outward below to form rounded, womanly hips, and tapering upward to breasts that looked far fuller than he'd at first thought, unfettered now by the snug fitting gown that she'd worn.

He had been staring blankly at her face for several moments, fighting the urge to mount her right then and there when it finally penetrated his heat fogged brain that the heat in her eyes was not the desire his mind had conjured as desire but one of pure rage.

A cold douse of water could not have more quickly, or thoroughly, dashed the fire in his blood.

It left him so quickly, in fact, that the rush was almost as dizzying as the rush *to* his brain and cock had been, and far less pleasant.

Slowly, as his brain kicked in and began to function once more, rage began to seep into him. "Reyhan!" he bellowed, so loudly that the sound ricocheted deafeningly off the stone walls, floor, and ceiling.

"Sire?"

Whirling, Talin fixed the hapless guard with a narrow eyed glare. "Come here."

Looking like he would've far preferred to make a dash for the door, the guard approached Talin and knelt.

Talin reached down, grabbed the man by his throat and lifted him to his feet. "Where are the princess' clothes and why is she not wearing them?"

Reyhan's jaw sagged. He glanced from Talin to Aliya and back again. "We always strip the prisoners," he stammered weakly. "To ... uh ... search them for weapons."

Talin ground his teeth. "Did I tell you she was a prisoner?" he asked, his voice deceptively soft now.

"Uh ... Sire? Uh ... no, Sire. But you said put her here. I thought ... I thought...."

"And the manacles?"

Reyhan blinked several times as the words pelted him in the face. "You said to make certain she couldn't injure herself."

"Which led you to believe this was necessary?" Talin ground out, releasing his hold on the man's throat and gesturing toward the manacles.

The man's eyes were bulging from their sockets. "She fought me like a wild thing when I tried to remove her clothing--took off half my hide with her nails and teeth. She injured herself injuring me! I thought the manacles would be bes--"

The last word remained incomplete. Talin belted Reyhan in the mouth with his fist so hard the man flew backwards, slamming into the wall behind him. Blood spattered the wall. Several teeth ricocheted off the wall and pinged onto the floor. Apparently satisfied when the man slumped to the floor and went still, Talin stepped over to him, bent down to retrieve the ring of keys from his belt and moved back to unlock the manacles.

Stunned by the turn of events, Aliya's anger vanished the moment Talin's erupted, tamped by a well developed, and heretofore unknown to her, instinct for survival. More than half fearing his anger would spill over onto her, she merely watched warily as Talin unlocked the manacle from first one wrist and then the other. A cry of pain was wrenched from her before she could prevent it, though, as her arms dropped limply to her sides and the blood began to flow through them in a stinging, burning tide.

Kneeling in front of her, Talin took one of her hands and gently massaged her arm. When he was satisfied, he lowered that arm and repeated the process with her other arm. More than a little disconcerted, Aliya watched him warily as he rose, looked around and finally strode to the corner where the guard had discarded her gown. After studying it critically for a moment, he shook his head and returned with it, helping her to her feet.

Pain shot through her knees and ankles the moment she rose, for she'd been kneeling on the hard stone for what had seemed like hours and hours. Gritting her teeth, she locked her knees and stood docilely while Talin pulled her gown over her head, adjusted it and haphazardly laced the back.

She was still trying to decide if she could actually walk without hobbling around like a crippled elder when he scooped her into his arms and turned toward the corridor. She stiffened. She wasn't certain she quite dared display her anger over her treatment at his hands now that she'd seen his temper, but she saw no reason to delude him into thinking she was anywhere near forgiving him for what he'd done to her--and ordered that son of a pig swiller to do.

She supposed, if she were to be reasonable about the matter--which she wasn't particularly inclined to be--she would have to admit that he did not *appear* to have had any notion of what the man would do. On the other hand, if he had cared to check before now she would not have been tortured for hours upon hours with her knees grinding into the hard stone and her arms withering from blood loss.

"I can walk on my own," she muttered through gritted teeth as he reached the main level of the castle and stalked down the corridor that led to the great hall.

The words were hardly out of her mouth when he dropped her feet to the floor. Resisting the urge to glare at him, she focused on trying to keep step with him as he grasped her by one arm and strode to the middle of the hall.

"Solly!" he bellowed, his voice still eloquent of fury even if his rigid countenance and heightened color hadn't been enough to assure anyone that saw him that he was in a towering rage.

Aliya clapped her hands over her ears, but jerked them down again when he sent her a searing glance.

"Sire!" Solly, ashen faced, knelt hurriedly, having virtually run across the hall at the bellowed summons that had made the crystal in the overhead chandelier tinkle merrily.

Talin gestured in the general direction of the dungeon. "Seize that fool, Reyhan, take him into the courtyard, and remove the remainder of his hide with a whip."

Guilt coiled tightly in Aliya's belly as the guard flicked a quick glance at her, nodded, and rose, summoning several guards and heading purposefully toward the dungeon and the unconscious man who lay there--unless he'd come around and had the presence of mind to flee while he could.

She didn't know why *she* felt guilty! It was not *her* fault the man was a fool, or his master so ill tempered!

She forgot the discomfiture of guilt, however, when Talin turned and headed toward the tower stair they'd descended before. In vain, she tried to put on brakes. She'd had more than enough time to relive those moments in the tower many times and she could only conclude that the fear had, temporarily at least, turned her mind. She knew very well that, as a princess, she should embrace death before dishonor, and if she could think of some way to do so short of taking a leap off the tower balcony she might be able to gather the courage to do so, but she rather thought she would prefer that he kill her now than to take her up there again. Everything inside of her clenched at the thought of being surrounded again by sky and space. Even the stone walls had seemed shaky and insubstantial when virtually all that met her gaze in any direction she looked was clouds and air.

She could not endure it, she thought a little wildly. She would die of pure fright.

Talin halted when he finally became aware that her feet, instead of moving, were skidding along the stones. Turning, he frowned at her curiously.

Aliya threw caution and dignity to the wind. "Kill me now! Just kill me! Do not torture me. I can not bear it. Truly, I can not!"

Talin looked as if she'd slapped him. The moment the look of stunned incomprehension left his face, though, he reddened with both anger and embarrassment. Hauling her against his chest, he glared at her nose to nose. "If you screech at me one more time, wench, I might well be tempted to throttle you!"

"Do it," she babbled, far more fearful of the terrible height than she was of his terrible temper. "I won't go up there! I won't!"

Uttering a growl that was one part anger and two parts frustration, he grabbed her around the waist and hauled her over his shoulder. Stunned, the breath knocked from her by the hard shoulder she landed on, Talin was halfway up the spiral stairs by the time she recovered enough to begin to struggle.

"NO! You fiend! You animal! Put me down! Put me down this instant!" she screamed, pounding on any part of him she could reach.

He smacked a hand against her buttocks. The sting wasn't nearly as potent as her stunned surprise and dawning outrage. However, before she could vent her indignation, he reached the top of the long, winding flight of stairs, crossed a short corridor and stepped through an arch, setting her abruptly on her feet.

She was in the tower room, she knew, and squeezed her eyes shut, afraid even to move. The slamming of a wooden door against stone frame work sent a jolt through her and she opened her eyes as she felt herself wavering and in danger of falling. To her stunned surprise, the room was cloaked in gloom save for branches of candles placed here and there.

It was night?

Feeling slightly better, Aliya pivoted slowly where she stood, her gaze searching the walls for window embrasures.

Shutters, she discovered, had been fastened over each and there was a door leading to the balcony where before there had been nothing at all! Relief flooded her that was so profound it brought stinging tears to her eyes and nose. She sniffed them back, glancing around warily for Talin when she remembered she'd fought him all the way up the stairs.

He was leaning against the door, his arms crossed over his broad chest, an indecipherable expression on his face.

Feeling sheepish, she sent him a faintly apologetic look. "I thought … I thought...."

His lips thinned. "I know what you thought."

Surprise went through her. "You do?" she asked doubtfully.

Shoving away from the door, he moved slowly toward her. "Yes."

Abruptly, Aliya realized he must think she'd been fighting for her virtue, when the truth was that her maidenhead was the furthest thing from her mind. She'd already opened her mouth to inform him of that when it occurred to her that she didn't especially want to disabuse him of the notion that she preferred death to ravishment by man beast.

She knew she should.

She was ruined now, whether he took her maidenhead or not, for no one would ever believe he hadn't and no one would want her. It would have been bad enough if he was merely a man, but he wasn't and that would make it that much worse.

She wasn't completely certain of how it could possibly be any worse, but she knew it would be.

"You are not as repulsed by me as you would have me believe," he murmured, halting mere inches from her and brushing the backs of the fingers of one hand lightly along her cheek.

He'd noticed that? She thought, feeling embarrassment pulse in her cheeks, flushing them with heat--which she very much feared he would notice and misinterpret as desire. "Your arrogance is only surpassed by your ego, Sire," she murmured tightly.

"And yet you didn't deny it."

Aliya gave him a look. "You would be deaf to it," she said, discovering that she felt vaguely breathless by his nearness.

He caught her hands, pushing them behind her back and drawing her closer. She twisted her face away, presenting him with her neck. "I suppose you think that you have only to kiss me and I will swoon and beg for more," she gasped, trying to swallow when her mouth had gone dry.

He nipped her earlobe, his heated breath teasing her ear and sending currents of sensation through her that seemed to sharpen her awareness of him. His scent filled her nostrils, teased her tongue with his taste. His heat cloaked her. The hard muscles of his body tantalized her, barely brushing her with each frantic breath she took. "You may keep your kisses if it pleases you to withhold them," he whispered against her ear, catching both of her wrists in one hand and lifting the other to push the shoulder of her gown down. "I had something else in mind."

Feeling strangely weak and light headed, Aliya was scarcely aware of any purpose to the stroke of his hand along her skin until she felt him dip beneath her bodice and cup one rounded breast. She gasped then, stiffened, trying to draw away as he lifted it from her bodice, but it was too late. His mouth settled over the distended tip, closed tightly upon her flesh. Her belly clenched as he sucked it, teasing her nipple with his tongue. Heat, like molten fire flowed through her, pouring into her lower belly and spawning a strange sense of excitement and need.

"S..stop," she finally managed to whisper shakily, although by that time she wasn't at all certain she wanted him to stop.

He ignored the command, continuing to suckle and tease her breast until she'd begun to feel as if she would faint. When he finally lifted his head to look at her, disappointment flooded her and it took all she could do to lift her eyelids to look back at him.

"As you please," he murmured, straightening.

Aliya stared at him blankly, feeling curiously bereft that he'd stopped.

"No doubt you're tired. I will send a maid to help you to bathe and prepare for bed," he murmured, releasing her and stepping away.

Still confused, feeling achy and oddly discomfited, Aliya merely stared at him. Finally, uncomfortable beneath his gaze, she turned away, looking around the great room at the sparse furnishings--for it contained little besides the huge bed in the center, an odd assortment of chests and tables, and a single chair. "I have no clothes," she murmured, feeling suddenly lost and more alone that she could ever recall in her life.

"I will send for your belongings in a few days. In the meanwhile, I'm sure the maids can find something for you. Are you hungry?" he asked abruptly when she merely turned and stared at him blankly.

"You will send for my belongings?"

He shrugged. "Aye. When the army your father is amassing moves off. I've no desire to lose good men gathering your trinkets."

Aliya felt her jaw sag. He had dismissed her father and his army as with no more than a shrug for the inconvenience to himself? Abruptly, all of the emotion she'd been holding at bay flooded into her in a chaotic storm. She was too enraged to think of anything to say, however.

Turning away when she remained mute, he strode toward the door they had entered but paused there, turning to glance at her again. Abruptly, as his gaze raked her bodice, Aliya became aware of her dishabille and grasped the shoulder of her gown, straightening the bodice and covering her breast. His lips thinned. "The shutters are bolted as well as yon door."

Aliya glanced at them, realizing belatedly that he had not covered them for her comfort but to make sure she couldn't make another attempt to destroy herself.

The arrogant cad!

"I don't care for them," he added thoughtfully. "Perhaps over the next few days you can entertain yourself with creating a design the carpenters can carve into them?"

At the comment, Aliya turned from her contemplation to look at him again, allowing a faint smile to curl her lips. "I would rather entertain myself with the design I would like to carve into your hide," she said with false sweetness.

His brows rose, but in a moment a smile curled one corner of his well etched lips. Instead of commenting on the episode between them a few moments before, however, as she more than half feared he would, he merely said, "You will stay here."

"And where will you be staying, your grace?"

His smile flattened. "Here."

"Then you may want to consider sleeping in armor."

He didn't look the least disconcerted by the threat. He seemed to consider it, but finally shook his head. "I prefer to sleep naked," he murmured, his golden eyes glinting with both humor and promise. Turning then, he quit the room before she could gather the presence of mind to find something to hurl at him.

Chapter Six

If Aliya had given it any thought, she would have been certain that she was not only not hungry but that the thought of food alone was enough to make her feel ill after all she'd been through. She discovered, though, that her stomach wasn't as delicate as her sensibilities. The maids arrived as promised, one with a tray of food and another with a stack of folded fabric that Aliya rightly assumed was the clothes that were on loan until Talin could have her 'trinkets' fetched.

That rankled. It was bad enough to be kidnapped by the spawn of the underworld gods and to be held against her will, but to have her needs and comfort dismissed as nothing more significant than 'trinkets' made her feel just as insignificant. If he had such a low opinion of her, she couldn't imagine why he'd gone to such trouble.

Unless it had been sheer contrariness and the desire to create disharmony?

She could easily have believed that, except that she couldn't think of any reason at all why he'd want to pick a fight with her father.

She was inclined to dismiss the 'great insult' he claimed. He was certainly very proud. She could see that, but he considered all of the unnaturals, himself in particular, to be far superior to the naturals. He had as much as said that he did not consider her worthy of being his queen, and that being the case it seemed unreasonable to *also* be insulted by anything the 'lesser' beings beneath him did.

Why should he care that he'd been excluded?

Dismissing it after a time as an unsolvable riddle, she ate the food that had been brought, enjoying it far more, she felt, than she should have under the circumstances, and watched while the maids brought in a tub and prepared a bath.

Her belly clenched in dread.

She wanted a bath. More than that, she needed one after all the time she'd spent in that devil's dungeon, but he'd ensconced her in his suite. She could not be certain that she would have privacy to bathe and she was fairly sure that, if it was possible to die of mortification, she would if he came in and watched.

She was very torn. The other considerations aside, she felt her dignity had suffered a very great deal already and it went against the grain to allow him to know just how scared she was about the entire situation and how unnerved she was about the possibility of being observed in her bath. She wanted to present a façade, at least, of royal unconcern--perhaps even disdain.

By the time she'd finished eating and the bath was prepared, she'd decided she would have her bath and to hell with the man--beast--whatever. She was sore from everything that had happened, and dirty, and tense. A hot bath would go a long way toward improving her outlook.

She was tense, though, while the maids helped her undress and then assisted her into the tub. Vaguely relieved that he hadn't suddenly appeared in the midst of that part of the process, she found she still couldn't relax and actually enjoy the bath. Instead, she rushed through it, hopping out as soon as she'd bathed and grabbing the drying cloth to wrap herself.

She discovered then that the only 'clothing' the maids had brought for her was night dresses. Shock very quickly gave way to anger, but it was already too late. The maids had taken her gown away and, when she demanded to have it back, explained that it was already in the laundry since they thought she might want to wear it the following day.

It sounded reasonable enough, but Aliya still wanted to strangle the maids. Unfortunately, that would not change her dilemma--sit around in nothing more than a thin cloth? Or sit around in nothing more than a thin night dress? She finally opted for one of the night dresses for the simple reason that she could at least put that on and wouldn't have to worry about trying to hold it together.

When she was dressed, she dismissed them, moving across the room to settle in the chair while they removed the bath, cleaned the room, and finally left her to her solitude.

Once they'd gone, she sat for a time smoothing the roughly woven fabric over her lap and trying not to think of anything at all. Idleness bred thought, though, and she found herself wondering about the strange land she'd found herself in, and most particularly the king of the tribe of golden falcon, Talin.

No one needed to tell her Talin had no layman in the castle. The gowns were of such poor quality it was obvious they belonged to the maids--unless he did have a mistress, but she'd refused to give up anything for the master's 'new whore'?

Not that she cared. He could have a hundred mistresses! A thousand!

The bastard!

She frowned at that thought, vaguely uneasy as to why she cared enough to even disapprove--most men had them and kings were most certainly no exception. Although her father was very discrete, she knew he had several and had probably had them even before her mother had died.

It almost seemed strange, though, to find herself comparing him, and his behavior, to her father, or any of the nobles she knew for that matter.

He was an unnatural. She had never thought to be around one. To everyone she knew, they were looked upon as nightmare creatures barely human at all. Most folk believed they were the spawn of the gods of the underworld, devils, demons, fiends--and she supposed she had, too.

She hadn't expected that they could look so--human! She supposed it was to be expected that they would assume a pleasing form when they walked about as humans, but they shouldn't have been *able* to when they were evil creatures. They should look evil to make it easier for *real* people to tell what they were.

Now that she had met Talin, she had to wonder how often these devils walked among them, completely undetected.

That was almost the most unnerving part of her situation. Talin walked and talked and looked and acted like any natural, and the more time that passed, the more difficult it was for her to keep the terrifying image of him in his beast form in her mind, particularly since she'd gotten little more than a glimpse of him in that form to start with.

She found herself reacting to him and interacting with him as if he was a real human. She'd fought him, argued with him, cursed him--threatened him even, as if, in the back of her mind, she'd still believed that her position was some sort of protection.

Worse, it seemed abundantly clear to her when this was the case after less than a full day that she was going to be deeply under the spell of his deception before long. She did not find him repulsive, as she knew she should, far from it. Before she'd known what he was she'd thought him very handsome, dangerously attractive. Now, even knowing dangerous was the key word, she was almost as drawn to him by his dangerous appeal as she was unnerved by it.

Did any of that truly matter, though, she wondered? What could she possibly do to keep him from taking what he'd made it clear he wanted? If he had been a natural born man, she could not have fought him off. The unnaturals were far stronger than their human counterparts.

That thought instantly conjured what he'd done to her earlier.

And the memory resurrected the sensations she'd felt before.

She'd done her best not to think about any of that since he'd left. The maids had been a welcome distraction, making it easier for her to do so, but it was an issue she couldn't continue to ignore.

He'd taken liberties with her that no one ever had before. He would almost certainly take more than that small taste of his possession.

It occurred to her that she hadn't been trying to avoid thinking about it because it had been so shocking, but because her reaction to it had been. Something had stirred to life inside of her when he'd touched her that she didn't want to face. She wasn't completely certain of what that something was, but, search though she might, she couldn't find so much as a trace of revulsion.

Shame began to trickle inside of her and ended in a flood when she realized that she'd been as fascinated and intrigued by his shocking behavior as she had been stunned and debilitated.

She frowned at that thought, trying to decide exactly how she had felt. Strange probably described the sensations best, because she'd never felt anything quite like it. There had been guilt, too, because he had touched her so intimately and she knew that was wrong when he wasn't her husband, and yet she was very much afraid that that was part of her fascination--experiencing the forbidden.

She couldn't remember a time when she had not been surrounded by women whose job it was to attend her needs and also to protect her from the things she, as a maiden, was not supposed to know. She'd been curious, though. When her body had begun to change, her mind had also and she'd found herself wanting to know those things forbidden for her to know, and to experience some of the things whispered around her when they thought she either couldn't hear, or wouldn't understand.

It had been easy enough to find out about kissing. With so many men and women living in the castle she had caught glimpses of couples entwined many times, their lips locked together and expressions on their faces that she'd first thought was pain. She'd felt like a fool when she realized that it was that elusive something called passion, but other than that she'd discovered very little.

Kissing, she'd been told, was the first step to ruin. She was not to even allow so much as that--if any man so forgot himself as to try it--because it would lead to 'more.'

Ladies were supposed to be pure of mind and body, and that was even more critical for a young girl who would one day be queen. She was to focus upon affairs of state, to concentrate her energies on learning what would be required of her as mistress of a kingdom. The marriage bed was only incidental to her station, since she would be required to produce heirs for her husband.

But no one had considered it important to explain to her just how she was to go about that most important task. The only thing she'd been told was that it was 'natural' and she would know what to do when the time came. She would have her husband's guidance to help her.

Feeling abruptly restless and vaguely angry, she got up from the chair where she'd been sitting for so long that she'd begun to ache with the inactivity and began to pace.

Her ignorance was no protection to her now. Talin had seemed downright amused by her refusal to kiss him. Obviously, *not* kissing him wasn't going to prevent him from doing 'the thing,' that vague 'something' that she knew men and women must do to produce heirs that took place behind closed doors and involved tussling about and moaning and groaning.

She'd only stumbled upon that part of the 'forbidden knowledge' once, and she hadn't been able to get up the nerve to try to peek and see what they were doing, but she'd heard and she'd known instinctively, as she'd been told she would, what was going on. Or rather, she'd gotten a general idea of what must be happening, for her mind had conjured images of the couple writhing against one another and kissing--which she knew was what started the rest.

Thinking about what they were doing, she realized suddenly, had made her feel just as she'd felt when Talin had kissed her breast, warm and strange and vaguely guilty.

Her belly tightened at the thought and fear of the unknown began to wrestle with the other sensations. He'd promised he wouldn't harm her, but she distinctly recalled that she'd seen more than one maid weeping after she'd disappeared with her swain one evening. Later, most of them had seemed to recover. Some had even seemed happy, almost deliriously so, but she hadn't been able to get the weeping out of her mind, or the sense that the maidens were maiden no longer, and that they were hurt, physically and emotionally.

Realizing she was scaring herself, Aliya struggled to put that from her mind. Thinking about what she was facing wasn't helping, for all she could do was pace faster in an effort to outrun her thoughts.

Growing tired after a while, she stared at the bed longingly for several moments and finally moved back to the chair.

Maybe she couldn't prevent it from happening to her, but she was NOT going to climb into the bed and lie there as if she was meekly awaiting her fate!

Hours passed, or so it seemed. Alternately pacing and resting in the chair, Aliya listened in vain for the heavy tread outside the door that would tell her the agonizing wait was over and she would have to face the unknown. She grew more and more tired. Finally, despite her anxiety, she found her eyelids growing heavy with the need to sleep.

Curling up in the hard chair, she shifted and squirmed, trying to find a comfortable position and finally dozed off.

The candles had guttered out when she woke and the room lay in darkness save for the thin streams of light that found their way between the planks that made up the shutters and door. Still drugged with sleep, she shifted, trying to ease the pain from her cramped position and finally sat up and peered at the bed.

It was empty.

It looked so inviting that she finally struggled to her feet, staggered to the bed and crawled in. At once, a vaguely familiar scent wafted up to her from the pillow she plumped under her head. Feeling comforted for no particular reason that she could figure out, she relaxed and sought oblivion once more.

The whisper of voices, the soft scuff of feet along the floor stones, and the faint tinkling of china woke her. For several moments, her mind simply accepted the familiarity of it. Slowly, awareness came to her that none of the voices she heard were the least familiar to her and she managed to crack one eyelid to see what was going on around her.

Uneasiness pierced the dregs of sleep that still enveloped her when she saw nothing familiar. There were no bed hangings to protect her from drafts and annoying insects. The mounds of pillows she was accustomed to were gone as well, leaving only the lumpy one beneath her head. The coverlet she was huddled beneath was of good quality, but the color was dull, more brown than gold, and certainly not the cheerful pattern of purple flowers that should have covered her.

With dread dawning, she slowly pushed herself upright and looked around the room in time to see the last of the maids departing.

Glumly, she looked around the tower room as her changed fortunes sank into her fully. As nightmarish as the day before seemed to her now, it was, unfortunately, reality, not the frightening dream that she'd hoped it was.

She'd already laid back down and pulled the covers over her head before it dawned on her that she'd been sleeping in Talin's bed. In her haste to evacuate, she tangled her legs in the bedding and sprawled in the floor.

The fall seemed to rattle her brain. For several moments, she lay still, evaluating the level of pain she could feel. Finally, she pushed herself up and managed to get to her feet.

The maids, she saw, had brought in fresh water and a tray of food. When she'd assured herself she was still in the room alone, she moved to the pitcher and basin that had been brought to her and washed her face and teeth.

She wasn't accustomed to eating in the morning and an odd mixture of hunger and nausea washed over her as she smelled the scent of food. After a moment's thought, though, she decided to see if she could eat anything. She felt weak and uncommonly weary, and the urge to climb back into bed and go back to sleep was strong. She reminded herself that she had no desire to be caught in Talin's bed--not by Talin.

The hot tea, she discovered, went a long way toward reviving her. Nibbling on a scone, she settled in the chair and looked around the room thoughtfully, wondering what seemed out of place.

It occurred to her finally, that it wasn't that anything was out of place, but that something she'd expected to find wasn't there.

Her lips tightened. The maids had told her they'd taken her gown to lauder it. They hadn't brought it back.

Slamming her tea cup back on the tray so hard she was a little surprised it didn't shatter, she surged to her feet and searched the room, knowing even before she did so that it was unlikely her dress would turn up.

It didn't. The chests in the room contained nothing but men's clothing--Talin's clothes. Slamming the lip of the last closed, she looked around the room for a bell pull to summon the maids and discovered there wasn't one.

She supposed that accounted for Talin's tendency to bellow for servants when he wanted them.

She glared at the door for some time, fighting the urge to march over to it and pound on it until somebody came. At best, such a thing would probably be useless since she doubted she could pound, or scream, loud enough to be heard over the din no doubt going on down in the great hall. At worst, it might bring Talin himself.

She moved back to the chair. The maids would come back, she assured herself, to remove the tray. When they did, she would give them a piece of her mind if they didn't have her gown when they came.

The food grew cold. Her anger dissipated at roughly the same rate as the heat from the food, and without that to sustain her, weariness set in.

She'd had very little sleep, she knew, and the activities of the day before had already strained her physically and emotionally. Realizing that she was going to nod off in the chair if she continued to sit, she got to her feet and began exploring the room.

There wasn't much to explore. She'd already rifled through all of the chests and not only had she not found anything in any of them of any interest, but she didn't particularly want to risk being caught plundering through Talin's personal belongings.

The only conclusion anyone could draw from such an action would be that she was searching for something to steal, or more interested in Talin than she had any desire for anyone to think.

Moving to the door that led into the corridor, she put her ear against it, listening. In the distance, she could hear the murmur of voices, but she couldn't hear well enough to tell what was being said.

Tiring of that fairly rapidly, she left the door and paced the room a while and finally returned to the chair.

She wasn't just scared anymore, she realized. In fact, at the moment, she wasn't fearful at all.

She was bored.

Sighing, she glanced around the room dully.

She missed her ladies. They had been chosen to serve her and she was not supposed to encourage them to treat her as an equal rather than their superior, but she had come to think of Lady Leesa and Lady Beatrice as friends and companions. They had filled the dark well of loneliness that had seemed an almost constant companion throughout her childhood and banished the sense of isolation she'd felt from the rest of the world with their talk of their own lives. Even the other maids, although she had not felt the same sense of closeness, had livened her days with their idle chatter.

The quiet that surrounded her now was suffocating.

She missed her apartment--all the things she'd taken for granted, even the tasks she'd once dreaded and found boring.

She missed her garden even more.

Strictly speaking, it wasn't her garden. Her father had had it designed and built for her mother, who had been from a land warmer than their own and had missed the garden of her childhood home. When she'd come of marriageable age, she had inherited her mother's apartments, and her mother's garden--which had been off limits to her as a child and which had gone to seed after her mother's death.

She had filled much of her days tending the plants and coaxing them to flourish once more, and a good part of her leisure there as well, working upon some needlework project or another and listening to her ladies talk about their homes, and their beaux.

She was never going to see her home again, or her garden, she realized with a shock of dismay.

She would've had to leave it anyway, when she was wed, but she would have been able to visit at least occasionally.

She would not be welcome there now. Her father would disown her. She'd sunk so low, her own people would probably spit on her.

Unwilling to go there, Aliya returned her thoughts to her garden, thinking back to what it had looked like when she'd first taken it as her own.

It occurred to her after a moment that, at first, she'd been unsettled by the fact that the garden was on a rooftop. It had seemed so very high that she couldn't bring herself to go near the low wall that surrounded it without feeling as if she was going to plunge to her death.

She'd forgotten that.

Over time, she'd grown so accustomed to the height. She'd ceased to find it unnerving at all!

It was a small step from that thought to wondering if she could grow accustomed to the terrifying height of Talin's castle.

Chapter Seven

Aliya turned to stare at the thin beams of light pouring through the shutters for several moments. Girding herself, she stood after a moment and moved to window. Her belly tightened before she'd even reached it and for several moments she paused, wondering if it was even a worthwhile idea.

She should try, she finally decided. Perhaps, even if she did grow more accustomed, it would mean nothing more than that she wasn't so on edge about the distance to the ground, but in the back of her mind she knew that as long as she was terrified of the height, she couldn't even search to see if there was a way to escape.

It seemed doubtful there would be. But wasn't some chance better than none?

Wasn't hope better than hopelessness?

Inching a little closer, she finally leaned toward the crack where the two planks of the shutter didn't completely meet and peered through it. Instantly, as her vision focused, her belly did a free fall and it felt as if her heart wasn't far behind it. Her chest felt as if it was wedged in a vise that was slowly tightening and squeezing the air from her lungs.

"They're bolted."

Aliya jerked all over at the abrupt intrusion having been so focused on her fear of the view beyond the window she hadn't even heard the door open. Sucking in a sharp inhalation of air, she whirled toward the sound, one hand lifting instinctively to the wooden panel to balance her.

A wave of dizziness went through her at the sudden movement.

Talin frowned, studying her with a mixture of anger and confusion. He could see she wasn't merely startled, however. She was shivering as if she was freezing.

There was something about her expression and the way she glanced back at the window and then moved away from it that gave him pause. After a moment, he crossed the room and stood where she had moments before, staring through the small crevice.

He could see nothing. He knew his own sight was far better than hers, so it could not be anything beyond his view that had disturbed her. Pulling away from the window, he turned to study her for several moments and finally glanced at the view again. Enlightenment dawned and yet he could hardly credit it.

"You are afraid of the height?"

Aliya stared at him mutely for several moments, but she could think of no reason to deny it. "I can not fly," she said stiffly. "I have never been so high above the world."

Some of the tension eased from Talin at that comment, and the roiling, sick anger that had been eating at him eased slightly.

He was almost tempted to smile. One look at her face was enough to assure him that would be poorly received, but he was relieved beyond measure that she had not, apparently, reserved that look of sheer horror for him. Frowning, he thought back over it and realized that she had hardly even glanced at him before when she was so terrified, and she had certainly shown no compunction about fighting him when he'd brought her to the tower again.

That had been because of her fear of the view, he decided.

Perhaps not all of it, he thought wryly, remembering what she'd said to him when she had discovered the door and windows were covered. She had seemed relieved about the shutters, but no more receptive to him.

He supposed it was something, at least, that she was more afraid of the height than she was of him.

Inwardly, he sighed. He was not generally such a numbskull, or so impulsive. If he had been a man child, she would have every reason to fear and loathe him for stealing her away. The fact that he was not only made it worse, not better, for he knew the man children despised and feared those they called the unnaturals. He felt a sense of hopelessness for the situation. No matter what he did now, he could not take back the way they had begun. The best he could hope for was that she would grow accustomed and come to accept and even that was bound to be an uphill battle.

She was attracted to him, even though it was obvious she loathed herself for it. He hadn't imagined that. As innocent as she was, she had responded to his touch readily.

Dismissing that thought abruptly when he felt the blood begin to surge through his veins, he focused on what he'd come for--a change of clothing.

At least he hadn't been so hardheaded, and stupid, as to press her right away, though the look of her naked form had sapped much of his sense straight down to his cock. Even thinking of it now made his blood surge and his cods tighten painfully. He glanced at her full lips with an insatiable hunger, then looked away and gathered his thoughts, steeling himself against the desire to take her.

It had taken distance from her to gain that much brain function, but he had realized that it would probably make things easier between them if he gave her time--at least a few days--to get over the worst of her fear and distrust.

He wasn't certain his patience would outlast more than a few days of being around her. She was his, regardless of how she might feel about that now, and his knowledge of that made it very difficult for him to control the beast inside of him that was clamoring to claim her in every way.

He'd stripped before it occurred to him that, as an innocent, his nakedness might discomfit her. When he glanced at her, he saw it had.

Her eyes were wide as saucers and she'd backed away until she'd come up against the wall. Frowning, he glanced down at himself, wondering if that look denoted interest or revulsion. He could see nothing about his man body--save the paleness of it perhaps--that she might find unappealing. His body was lean and not excessively hairy. He was not scarred. His muscles were well developed, perhaps a little too much, for they bulged, forming hard knots in some places and long ropes in others, but it was a warrior's body and she had wanted a warrior.

His man tool was flaccid. She could not be intimidated by that, although he was pleased himself to see that, even sleeping, it was a powerful looking beast and well proportioned to his body--maybe a little over large, but not freakishly so and he rather thought he preferred to err on size in that direction than the other.

After some consideration, he finally decided that she appeared more shocked than anything else--which meant that she had either never seen a naked man, or she was stunned to see he looked much like any man.

The last wasn't a particularly pleasing thought. It was disappointing only to see that glazed look in her eyes when he would've preferred to see admiration and lust, but he supposed the blank look was better than horror.

Sighing, he squatted in front of the chest at the foot of the bed, found the clothes he wanted and closed the chest again. She hadn't moved, he saw. Dropping the clothing on the bed, he headed toward the table that held the washbasin. To his surprise, Aliya slipped along the wall until she met up with the table and then turned and moved along the table, effectively blocking his access to it.

He paused in front of her, looking down at her upturned face with a mixture of desire, irritation, and amusement. The urge to tease her came out of no where. Dipping his head until his lips were no more than a hair's breadth from hers, he murmured, "Do you mind?"

She blinked. Her lips parted ever so slightly in surprise.

His mouth went dry. He swallowed with an effort, trying to decide if she was actually offering her lips to him. Deciding finally that she wasn't, that it was only wishful thinking on his part, he grasped her shoulders in his hands and set her to one side.

When he'd washed his face and teeth and dried himself, he glanced at her again and discovered she'd sidled down the wall in the other direction. She didn't look frozen, however. She looked embarrassed.

Resisting the temptation to tease her any more, he returned for his clothing and dressed. He was about to leave when she stopped him.

"My ladies? You did not harm them?"

He turned to study her, frowning slightly. "You saw that I did not."

Aliya's brow creased. "I thought--but I was not certain. I am ... very fond of them. Even if I was not, I would not want them to be hurt," she added hastily.

His lips flattened. "I do not harm those who can not defend themselves. And, in any case, I would not have harmed them for trying to defend you." He seemed to think it over for a moment. "I was pleased that they did. It told me much about you that I had heard was true."

Aliya looked at him questioningly, but he didn't elaborate. When she saw that he would go, she stopped him again.

"That ... uh ... the guard, Reyhan?"

"What about Reyhan?"

"Is he ... is he ... did he survive the whipping?"

His brows rose in surprise. "Of course. He is back at duty, but he will not soon forget the lesson."

Aliya frowned in confusion "He was whipped?"

"Yes. I ordered it."

"I don't understand. You said ... uh ... I would not have thought he would be well enough to return to duty so soon."

He studied her curiously. "Shall I have him come and show you the marks? It was done. No one ignores my orders with impunity."

Aliya shifted uncomfortably. "I was angry, but I didn't want him to die."

"There was never any possibility of it. If you knew anything about my people, you know that. The lesson was a painful one, not a death sentence. We feel pain, just as you do, but we heal quickly--most of the time."

Aliya nodded jerkily, finding that she was relieved. She'd meant it. As furious as she was to be treated in such a way, she would not have liked to think the man lost his life only because he had, apparently, misunderstood what he'd been told to do. She wasn't completely certain she believed he'd even been whipped. She had heard that the unnaturals were demons, and that was why it was nigh impossible to kill one, but that seemed less likely to be the truth to her now that she had met Talin. For how could they be so very like them and not be the same?

She hesitated when he turned to go once more, but she realized she would rather know than merely wait to learn her fate and worry over it. "What will happen to me?"

He had already opened the door, but at that he closed it once more and turned to face her again. "I will take you as my concubine."

Aliya felt a mixture of anger and fear. "Why? Why would you dishonor me?"

"I have not. I have not threatened to. You will be my concubine. That is a position of honor, second only to the queen."

Aliya swallowed against the knot of emotion in her throat. "I am a princess. Taking me without benefit of marriage would be to dishonor me."

"You will be my wife--my mate. It is all that I can offer to make things right. I could not make you my queen if I wanted to. My heir must be pure of blood. The council would never accept the offspring of a man child."

"Then take me back! Take me to my father, to live among my own kind--where I can wed one of my own kind and my children will be accepted."

"No."

She stamped her foot angrily. "Why? Why would you do this to me? I have done nothing to you! Is it to assuage your anger over the insult you think my father gave you?"

His brows dropped ominously over his eyes and his lips tightened. "Because I want you."

Chapter Eight

Aliya gaped at him in stunned dismay. Finally, her anger asserted itself once more. "This face? This body? What will become of me when I am no longer young and desirable to you? Will I be cast aside? Shamed? At least if I was allowed to marry among my own people I would always have the respect of my position!"

"You will have the respect of my people! It could not be otherwise, for I would not have it otherwise!"

Aliya stared at him dully, fighting the urge to shame herself by yielding to tears. He either didn't understand, or he was willfully ignoring the truth. She would not be looked upon by his people as his 'second' wife, but a glorified whore, and her own people wouldn't even consider her a king's whore--which at least had some status, for they loathed and feared the unnaturals and would only think of her as tainted beyond redemption, the cast off unworthy of even the creatures of the underworld.

When she said nothing else, he left her to her solitude, but there was little comfort in it. The barely acknowledged hope that she'd nurtured that he had not come to her the night before because he had reconsidered was quashed. She didn't know why he just didn't go ahead and take his pleasure and be done with it.

Was it some sort of diabolical torture? To allow her hour upon hour, perhaps days, to dread and wait for the inevitable?

She did dread it, but she discovered that boredom was a very effective remedy for fear. Cooped up in Talin's suite all day, she had nothing at all to keep her company beyond her own thoughts and nothing to look forward to except the maids who brought her food.

They didn't bring her gown. Each time she asked, they gave her an excuse instead of producing it. When it grew dark, one came and lit the candles, replacing those that had burned completely. After the evening meal, the maids trooped in again as they had the night before and prepared a bath, readied her for bed and departed again.

By the time she'd spent the following day in much the same way, she decided that she was going to go stark raving mad if she could do nothing but await her fate. She had never given much thought to what it must be like for the condemned, but she began to think she had a fair notion.

On the third morning when she woke, she discovered that when the maids had delivered her breakfast tray, they had also brought pen and ink and parchment. She ignored it for a while, testing herself against the view beyond the window and discovering she felt just as frightened and ill each time she looked. If she stood for a very long time without moving, focusing on one spot, some of the fear seemed to lessen, but she knew she was still a very long way from growing accustomed even to looking. The thought of trying to scale the distance to the earth below boggled the mind.

When she felt that she had endured as much 'growing accustomed' as she could bear, she moved away from that window. After a little thought, she moved on to another, and then another, wondering if there was anything she might see in any direction that would give her some hope.

She found that two of the windows looked down upon a flattened area in the center of the castle walls. Men, or what looked like men but what she knew must be unnaturals, were gathered there. Most were lined along the edges of the clearing, watching, but perhaps a dozen had been paired off and were exercising their skills with swords.

Was it merely practice, she wondered? Or were they drilling for war?

She was inclined to dismiss the last. Talin had said her father was making preparations for war, and she knew that he must be determined to rescue her. But she also knew, even if her father didn't, that he could not even reach the kingdom of the golden falcons, let alone wage war against them.

Talin would know that, too. He would have no reason to form up his army and prepare for a war.

Tiring of standing after a while, she moved to the chair to rest, studying the parchment.

Talin had suggested she 'entertain' herself by trying to design a pattern for the shutters. She supposed it was perverse, but she was reluctant even to try.

She was bored though, and it seemed better to focus her mind on something pleasant than to dwell on her fears. After a few minutes, she rearranged the chair, smoothed the parchment and then simply stared at it for a while, trying to conjure an image in her mind that she could try to draw. Slowly, the image of her rooftop garden began to form. She sketched the arbor that shaded the sitting area where she and her ladies often sat. When she'd finished, she studied the attempt, decided she was reasonably satisfied with it and began trying to add in smaller details.

She grew cramped, huddled over the page she was sketching on, but once she'd begun to see the image in her mind transformed onto the paper, she didn't want to stop. She drew the miniature fruit trees in huge pots that grew alongside the arbor retreat, the flowering vine that grew all over the arbor, dripping clusters of flowers. And when she had drawn everything that she could recall, she began to sketch herself and her ladies sitting among the cushions.

Try though she might, she couldn't capture their faces. Even her mind defied her there, for when she concentrated as hard as she could, she still couldn't quite visualize their features. She could remember the way they smiled and laughed. She could remember the times when her ladies squabbled among themselves about one thing or another, but she couldn't remember the shape of their faces, or their features. She couldn't remember how tall any of them were, or more than the general shape of their figures.

Had she forgotten so much already? Or had she never really looked at them at all? Or was it just that she was not talented or skilled enough?

Disappointed and far more depressed than when she'd started, she wadded the paper up impatiently and rose from the chair.

She had ink on her hands and forearms. She'd dripped ink on the gown she was wearing, as well, and when she lifted it, she saw the ink had soaked through into her skin.

She was as untidy as child!

She had ruined the night gown, she realized guiltily. She would have felt badly about it if it had been her own, but it wasn't. It belonged to someone else and as poor as she thought it was, it might well be the best that they had.

Perhaps it wasn't dried yet, though?

Moving to the washstand, she lifted the fabric away from her skin and dipped it into the basin. The dark stain spread, but she saw that some darkened the water, too. Taking the soap from the stand, she rubbed that into the ink and began scrubbing it.

The door opened behind her and she turned guiltily to see who it was.

Talin strode into the room, wearing nothing more than a narrow strip of linen wrapped haphazardly around his waste and dripping water.

Aliya stared at him, feeling her jaw go slack. It wasn't nearly as great a shock to see him the next thing to naked as it had been when he'd stripped to nothing, but she found she was far from immune.

Remembering the night before, she felt blood flush her cheeks with embarrassment. Averting her gaze, she struggled to focus on the task she'd set herself.

She was so busy ignoring him that it wasn't until the rattling of paper stopped that it dawned on her that he was looking at her attempt to draw.

Whirling abruptly, she saw that she was right. He'd straightened the sheet she'd wadded into a ball and was studying it, his face drawn into a frown, as if he couldn't quite figure out what it was supposed to be.

Embarrassment over her lack of talent superseded all other considerations. Before she'd even had time to think it over, she raced across the room to snatch it from his hands.

He heard her coming. Obviously, he also realized her intent. Even as she skidded to a halt and reached for the parchment, he snatched it off the table and held it out of her reach. "I was looking at it."

Aliya glared at him. "If I had wanted you to see it I would have shown it to you."

"If you had wanted it at all, you would not have tried to destroy it."

She made another grab for the paper, sprawling against him when he merely held it higher. She was so intent on getting her hands on it, in fact, that she'd wallowed all over him, grabbing the arm that held the sketch and putting every ounce of her weight on it to drag it down, before it dawned on her abruptly that he'd gone perfectly still.

When his stillness finally penetrated her focus on the sketch, she stopped abruptly. Before she could retreat, however, his free arm snaked around her waist.

Her heart flip flopped in her chest, making her feel breathless and more uncomfortably aware of her body plastered against his hard chest and belly.

"This is very good. Why would you want to destroy it?" he asked after a prolonged moment of silence.

She glared at him for the reminder. "It is very terrible. A child could do better," she snapped, shamed at the crude attempt and angry with him for seeing she had no more talent than that.

"If you meant to throw it away, you will not mind that I have it."

That comment effectively silenced her. She did mind, but it dawned upon her finally that she couldn't best him and take it away from him. The only think she could do to try to save face was to pretend indifference--something rather difficult considering she'd been bouncing all over him trying to take it back.

"Fine!" she retorted ungraciously. "Amuse yourself at my expense if that is the sort of thing you find entertaining!"

She shoved at his arm to free herself. Almost reluctantly, he released her, and she stalked back to the basin. Once there, she simply stared at the ink stained water in the bowl for several moments. As embarrassed and upset as she was about the drawing, she was shaken more by her awareness of him and the tingly feeling running all over her skin. Right up until the moment that she'd realized he had stopped trying to evade her, she'd been intent on retrieving the parchment and nothing else. In the next moment, her senses sharpened, focusing entirely on Talin so that her awareness of everything else vanished. The clean scent of freshly scrubbed body filled her senses first and then the dampness that still lingered on his skin, the sharp contrast of warmth and coolness emanating from his partially dry flesh, and the silken feel of his skin over taut muscles.

She hadn't even been able to span the circumference of his upper arm when she'd grasped it with both hands trying to tug his arm lower so that she could reach the parchment--or budge it with all her weight hanging upon it--and the muscle had felt as hard as the stone walls of the tower.

She had liked the way he'd felt against her body, she realized in dismay.

Her body seemed almost to sizzle even now, prickling as it sometimes did in the winter time when the heat of the hearth seemed to charge her hair and woolen garments with some strange energy.

She felt--expectant, oddly agitated.

Her womanhood felt hot and uncomfortably moist and as prickly aware as the rest of her, perhaps more so. For several moments, she fought back the nervous feeling assailing her, willing her breathing and rapid heartbeat to return to normal.

After a moment, she focused determinedly on rinsing the soap and ink from the gown, her ears pricked for any sound that might tell of his approach. She felt a little let down when he didn't and finally nerved herself to glance in his direction.

He was frowning, she saw, but she didn't think it was anger--nor concentration for that matter, although he was busy, she saw with relief, securing his breechcloth. For several moments, she was captured by that act, watching the play of muscles in his arms, trying hard to keep her curious gaze from examining the bulge in his breechcloth too keenly.

If she had not been so preoccupied with examining his body, she might have noticed sooner that he had both hands occupied. As it was, he'd finished and reached for another article of clothing before she realized he'd laid the parchment he'd stolen from her on the bed.

She averted her gaze. Lifting the hand cloth from the rung that held it, she brushed absently at the damp spot she'd made, trying to watch him surreptitiously out of the corner of her eye.

He'd picked up a pair of trousers. Surprised, she forgot she was trying to be sly and flicked a gaze at his face as he thrust one foot into the breeches he held up.

He was focused, she saw, on what he was doing.

If she had stopped to consider, she would have realized that the chance of snatching the parchment before he could react was slim at best. She acted on impulse, however, and the moment she burst into movement, his sharp, hawk-like gaze zeroed in on her.

Releasing his grip on the trouser, he caught her even as she tried to dart past and snatch the drawing. Before she could even inhale a startled gasp, she found herself lying flat of her back on the bed with Talin planted firmly on top of her. Too stunned to think, much less to fight, she gaped up at him, blinking as she sucked in a harsh, startled breath.

A slow smile began to curve his finely etched lips. Something gleamed in his eyes that was equal parts amusement and ... something else that seemed directly related to that serpent in his breechcloth, for it ... grew. And seemed to seek the heated crevice between her thighs as he prodded the top of her mound. "There was no need to assault me," he murmured. "If you are ready you need only say so."

Aliya felt her jaw sag. Discovering her mouth was bone dry, she licked her lips. His eyes slid half closed. He followed the movement of her tongue, his gaze watchful. "Ready?" she managed to ask weakly.

Almost reluctantly, he dragged his gaze from her mouth and met her eyes. "To join."

Aliya blinked again as if she'd never heard the word before. "Join what?" she asked in confusion.

A husky chuckle escaped him. He dropped his head, nipping at the tender skin of her neck. A rash of goose bumps pebbled her skin, spreading like wildfire down her chest and arms. She felt her nipples pucker into hard little knots and shifted uncomfortably, fearful that he would feel the rigid points.

He must have, for he began to wind a trail downwards with his lips. "Our bodies," he murmured, "in the mating dance. I am striving for patience, but I confess it is a struggle."

Aliya sucked in a breath and held it as he nuzzled the space between her breasts and began to climb toward one engorged peak.

A sense, almost of smugness, filled her when she realized his intent, for he had her wrists pinned to the bed on either side of his head. He could not hold her and use his hands, and *this* time she was fully clothed.

A jolt of stunned surprise went through her when he covered the tip with his mouth and suckled it. Even through the fabric the heat of his mouth and the teasing stroke of the tip of his tongue sent a rush of exquisite sensation through her, sucking the air from her lungs. "How ... how would we do that?" she said in a gasping voice, struggling to find something to distract him--to distract her own mind from the chaotic feelings surging through her.

The question had the effect of making him lift his head to look at her, but she realized it had been a mistake when he shifted, arching his hips against her. The long, hard ridge of flesh that dug into her mound sent a stunning jolt of heat through her. Almost as if in answer to some primal call of the flesh, she felt the muscles in her belly clench.

Enlightenment dawned like a cold douche of water. "Oh! No! I couldn't," she babbled. "It's ... uh ... it wouldn't fit. Would it?" It looked and felt impossibly huge and hard. She knew, of course, that women had babies and babies were bigger, but before the gods! Women died screaming, too.

His lips curled into a smile. "We can see."

"I'm not ready to see," she hissed, tensing all over and struggling to free herself.

He tilted his head curiously. "No? When will you be ready?"

Never! "I have to say?" she demanded, appalled at the idea.

"I could just guess."

That was even worse. She cast around her mind a little wildly for something she could say that would stave him off for a while. The only thing that came to mind was not something she wanted to discuss with him--or any man. "I--uh--I--uh .... It is not a good time ... now."

His brows rose questioningly and she felt a blush rising until it felt like her face was on fire.

"It's my woman's time," she blurted baldly.

He looked surprised for a moment, but only a moment. Then he began to look suspicious. "Liar," he murmured.

"Almost," she amended, without any idea whatsoever whether it was near her time or not.

After studying her for several moments, he shrugged and slipped off of her, tugging her up as he stood. "I will let it go ... for now."

Aliya was so relieved she felt almost faint. Nodding jerkily, she stepped away from him. As she did, her gaze flickered to her drawing.

Almost casually, he reached past her, grasped the piece of parchment and carefully rolled it into a tube. While she watched him, he took the roll, pulled the waist of his breechcloth away from his stomach and tucked the tube inside.

Aliya watched the entire proceedings with a mixture of dawning outrage and dismay.

When she looked up at him, she saw that Talin's eyes were dancing with merriment.

The devil! He hadn't believed for one moment that she couldn't contain herself! He'd known all along she was after that drawing, she thought indignantly.

Chapter Nine

Talin sprawled negligently on his throne, his left arm propped on one armrest, and his right leg hooked over the one on the opposite side as he studied the sketch he held in his hand thoughtfully. After a time, he dropped the parchment onto his lap and began to drum his fingers on the armrest beneath his hand, his gaze slowly scanning the great hall where most of his men were gathered.

They were a rowdy lot. Having spent most of the day bashing heads and pounding away at one another with swords, they were in great spirits, and pretty well into their cups if it came to that.

Spying his master carpenter near the rear of the hall, Talin waited until the man glanced his way and crooked an imperious finger at him.

Startled, Silo glanced to first one side and then the other. When he looked at his king questioningly, Talin crooked a finger at him again.

Certain he must be mistaken, he nevertheless crossed the room quickly and knelt before the throne, wondering if Talin had discovered something about the shutters and doors he didn't care for. "Sire?"

"I do not believe I know your name. Do I?"

The carpenter sent him a startled glance. "Silo, Sire."

"Are you merely a carpenter? Or are you also skilled in cabinet making?"

Silo glanced at his king uneasily. "I can do both, sire, but most folks think I'm best at designing cabinets and the like."

Talin nodded. Lifting the goblet he held in the hand he'd draped on his knee, he took a long draught, then tossed the vessel over his shoulder. "Tell me what you make of this," he said, lifting the parchment and holding it out.

Uneasy, particularly since he could see the king was a bit the worse for drink, Silo took the parchment, straightened the curling edges and stared at the black lines crisscrossing the page. Mayhap he'd had a bit too much to drink himself, for he could make nothing of it. Deciding he must have it upside down, he turned it around and studied it again.

Talin leaned forward to peer at the parchment. An expression of displeasure creased his features. Snatching it from Silo's hands, he righted the sketch and handed it back. "This way," he snapped irritably. "She is very talented," he added challengingly. "Only see how well she has captured it with nothing more than a pen and ink."

Silo stared at the line drawing, feeling sweat begin to pop from his pores when he found he couldn't tell much about the picture at all. Was it a design, he wondered uneasily? It didn't look like a cabinet. There seemed to be figures of women arranged over it. A carving?

Mayhap the drink had affected his vision, he decided, moving the parchment in and out of his focus until the lines didn't look quite so blurry. "It's quite nice, Sire," he said after a few moments of fumbling around in search of anything at all to say.

"But what do you make of it?"

Silo stared at his king unhappily. "It's a very good design. Very good," he responded somewhat hopefully, wishing he hadn't noticed the king motioning for him, or that he could somehow make an escape now.

Still drumming his fingers on the armrest impatiently, Talin lifted his other hand and began to stroke his lower lip thoughtfully. "I recognize this place," he said, as if he'd just come to a decision.

"You do?" Silo asked doubtfully.

"She was sitting there when first I saw her. What do you think that means?"

Silo's jaw dropped. For several moments his mind was perfectly blank. Suddenly, it dawned upon him that Talin must be talking about his princess. "Princess Aliya?" he asked carefully.

Talin glared at him. "Whom did you think I was talking about man? How much have you had to drink?" he added suspiciously.

"A pint," Silo responded weakly. "Mayhap two."

"Well, you can not hold your drink man!" Dragging his leg off of the armrest, he planted it on the floor and leaned forward. "This here is posts. There are several upright and then others sort of crisscrossing the top and there was a plant growing over it, a vine of some sort, pillows and such beneath to sit upon."

Silo scratched his chin, thinking frantically. Abruptly, a thought came to him. "An arbor?"

"Yes! That is the word I was looking for--an arbor, and benches below. There were many plants in pots sitting around."

"A garden?"

Talin thought that over. "Not the likes of which I have seen before. The dirt was all in pots. It was on a rooftop."

Silo nodded wisely. "How clever! Ladies love gardens. They are very fond of flowering things."

"Ah," Talin said, nodding and settling back in his chair. "You think that is what this means?"

Silo blinked several times. Mayhap the king was right, he thought. Mayhap he could not hold his drink well at all. He was certain he had had no more than two pints and in general he thought he held it well, but he could scarcely make heads or tails of anything the king was saying. "Uh … yes?" he responded hesitantly, having decided that it would be best to agree with King Talin, whatever it was he was talking about.

Doubt shook him when Talin's expression turned grim. "I thought as much. And we do not have one."

"I am certain we can remedy that, Sire," he said hastily, trying to soothe the brewing storm.

Talin glared at him. "You have magic that will make green things grow here? For I am certain it would take that. There are no trees so high up and no plants."

Silo gaped at the king, his mind scurrying around frantically for something to appease the man--whom he'd begun to think had been bitten by more than a touch too much to drink. "She misses her garden?"

"You said she did," Talin bellowed impatiently. "Why else would it be the first thing she thought of?"

"Oh. OH!" Silo exclaimed, everything suddenly becoming clear. "Oh!" he added when he realized that Talin was right. They had no garden in the palace because they could not grow things so high up. "I have no magic," he added a little uneasily, for he could see it was going to be all his fault that he could not perform a miracle to help Talin please his lady.

To his relief, Talin settled back in his chair, however, draping one knee over the armrest as he had before. Frowning, he glanced around the great hall as if seeking a new target for his wrath. Spying a servant, he bellowed for another pint of ale. Silo had just decided that he'd been dismissed when Talin focused on him again. "She will not smile for me," he said morosely. "Mostly, she will only stare at me as if I am a monster."

Silo gaped at his king, wishing Talin hadn't been inspired by drink to confide in him. He sincerely hoped that Talin would not later regret it. A happier thought occurred to him directly after that, that if Talin drank enough he might not recall the conversation at all.

He could see Talin expected a response, though, and he wasn't at all certain what sort of response would work to his advantage. In his experience, no one wanted the truth if it conflicted with what they wanted, and, unfortunately, he could see the lady's point. She was not the same as they, and she had been stolen from her home. No doubt she had been brought up to believe, as most man children were, that the man beasts were all monsters--more beast than creatures of intelligence. "She was not pleased with the shutters?" he asked finally.

Accepting the mug of ale the servant handed him, Talin took a draught. "She is not so terrified now. I can not see that she is especially pleased." It occurred to him that he hadn't done it to please her. He'd had it done to keep her from taking a fatal leap in order to escape his clutches. That realization didn't help his feelings a whit.

Silo nodded. "She was fearful of the height," he said wisely. "Not surprising, for she is only a man child after all and can not fly as we can. Naturally, she would fear falling."

Talin stared at the man in surprise for a moment. "You knew this?" he demanded.

Silo gaped at him. "I thought that was why you ordered me to affix shutters and doors."

Talin felt heat rise in his face. He averted his gaze to the liquid in his mug. "Aye. I was only surprised that you had figured it out when you had not had the opportunity to observe her."

Silo shrugged. "I was not certain. I say only that I am not surprised."

Talin frowned. "She did not seem particularly pleased when I told her I would send for her belongings. *You* seemed to think that would please her," he growled accusingly.

"I--uh--I only suggested that, perhaps, that would help her to grow accustomed--if she was surrounded by things familiar to her," Silo said, uneasy about disputing Talin, but certain that he would otherwise be blamed if it transpired that the princess was not pleased.

"Do not hedge, man!" Talin growled. "The situation is dire! The mating is upon me and my beast grows harder to quiet daily. How am I to go about gaining her acceptance?"

Silo gaped at him. "Sire! You can not claim a mate unless she is willing to be claimed! It is … not done!"

Talin ground his teeth. "I know this, but my beast does not care!" he growled.

"You only *think* that now," Silo retorted, greatly daring. "If she does not feel as you do, then she will turn from you when her true mate appears. And you will go mad."

"I am going mad now," Talin growled testily, beginning to drum his fingers on the armrest again.

"This is a very bad situation," Silo said thoughtfully. "You are wise to keep your distance from her just now," he added after a moment. "Allow her time to lose the worst of her fears and then she will be more receptive to the courtship."

Talin felt his face redden again. It wasn't wisdom, precisely, that had made him keep his distance. It was more the fear that he would go too far too fast and bungle the entire courtship. "I have reason to believe she does not find me completely distasteful," he muttered.

Silo brightened. "Well, and that is a start!" he said bracingly, but then frowned. "Of course, she is not one of the people. But I am sure it is a good sign if she does not try to shred your hide when ever you are around her. I am convinced you are on the right track. Certain of it! Once you have brought her belongings, she will be more comfortable. And she will see you are eager to find favor with her. I will put some thought into the garden you wish to give her." He frowned again. "Statuary, you think? I could not help but notice there were figures of women in the drawing."

"There were no statues," Talin said musingly and then brightened suddenly. "Her ladies! They are devoted to her and vice versa, I am certain. Mayhap it is not the garden she misses at all, but her ladies?"

Silo nodded. "No doubt! She is very alone now and not at all accustomed to being alone. I will study over this matter of a garden and see what I can come up with," he added, hoping the promise would be sufficient to appease Talin, for the moment anyway.

Talin nodded, flicking a hand at him in a shooing motion. Grateful to have the interview at an end, Silo scurried away. He was tempted to stop for another tankard, but after a very little thought decided against it. The king might decide he wanted to speak with him again and the conversation they'd already had had agitated him enough. He rather thought he would make himself scarce for a few days--more than a few if he could not come up with a solution to the problem Talin had presented him with.

* * * *

The more Talin considered the matter, the more certain he was that Silo was right about Aliya. A great part of Aliya's unhappiness was her loneliness. It would not be enough merely to lose her fear. She must be happy, comfortable. She needed *people* who were familiar to her, not just things.

Talin was beginning to think the elder's wisdom was of far more use to him than that of his council, for they were never in agreement over anything. In any case, he would not have wanted to approach them with this particular problem. For once, they had united--in disapproval over his actions. Not that they were against the war, or avenging the slight. They had, in fact, demanded that something be done. He had been more inclined to simply ignore it. After all, it was not even acceptable for him to take a mate outside his kind. What did he care if the man children comforted themselves in their weakness with the mistaken belief that they were somehow better than their superiors, the man beasts?

They had not been satisfied with merely ignoring it, however. They had gathered for weeks to argue over the best way to teach the man children a lesson, working themselves up to a fever pitch until he could see he would have no peace if he allowed the slight to go unchallenged.

In truth, he had found that he was intrigued after a time by the tales of the princess. Not one report indicated that she was less than perfection and the more he thought about that, the more indignant he was that he had not been considered suitable and the more certain he became that, if she truly was so exceptional, then she was far too great a prize to end up in the bed of some wizened old lecher who had the coin to hire the best warrior to compete.

He did not regret his decision. If the council members were less than enthusiastic over the manner in which he'd provoked the war they had been clamoring for, then that was their problem.

His beast had spoken. From the moment he had set eyes upon her, he had known that she was the one and that no other would do. He was willing to bow to tradition and choose a queen among their own people to produce the heir to his throne, but he would give no further. Aliya would be his concubine, the mate of his heart and soul. It could not be otherwise. His beast did not make that sort of mistake. Instinctively and inexorably, it was drawn to the female most perfect as his match.

Unfortunately, as a man child, she did not understand her own instincts. She relied upon emotion and logic to guide her when there was nothing at all logical about choosing the perfect mate.

He decided he would lead his men in the raid to retrieve those things she felt she had lost. He would know what was most important to her, after all.

Besides, his gift to her might not be as appreciated if he merely sent others to do his bidding. He wanted to be able to bask in the fullness of her joy and appreciation.

Chapter Ten

Princess Aliya would have liked to blame her restless night on most anything except the true reason she'd had so much difficulty sleeping, but she was not prone to trying to delude herself. She'd grown restless and achy every time she recalled the things that Talin had done to her and that strange neediness had invaded her dreams when she'd finally drifted to sleep.

She felt no better when she woke and wondered if there was any real reason to get out of bed as early as she customarily did. She was still tired and it wasn't as if she had anything of interest to occupy her time.

That thought promptly resurrected the incident with Talin and she flopped back on the bed, dragging a pillow over her head.

She didn't know which was worse, her reaction to Talin, or the fact that he'd been well aware that he'd stirred her blood.

He'd been well pleased with himself, too, she thought irritably, wishing she could have thought of something clever to give him a set down.

After a time she drifted to sleep again. When she woke the second time she felt considerably better. She saw when she tossed off the covers and sat up that the maids had been in, removed the breakfast tray, which she'd ignored, and left fresh water, and her gown!

Delighted to discover they'd returned it at long last, she slipped from the bed and went to examine it. It was a little the worse for wear, having lost a few of the tiny pearls sewn to it, but she saw it had been laundered and the wrinkles carefully ironed from it.

Settling it on the bed, she went to the basin to wash up. The maids returned as she was struggling to get into the gown by herself and moved to help. Removing it again, the younger of the two straightened her corset and tightened the laces, then drew the gown over her head again and laced the back up.

"Would you like for us to bring your noon meal up, or would you prefer to go down to the great hall?" the other maid asked.

She had a choice? She was heartily sick of her own company, but she felt a little uneasy at the thought of mingling with the unnaturals. Finally, she decided to have a tray brought up.

To her surprise, once she'd finished eating and the maids returned to retrieve the tray, they offered to escort her to the courtyard to enjoy the sun and fresh air. She was still a little uncomfortable about the unnaturals, but she discovered the chance to get out was just too tempting to pass up.

* * * *

Impatient to present Princess Aliya with the gift he'd thought of for her, Talin gathered a squad of men the following day and set out for the kingdom of Anduloosa. There was a possibility, he knew, that King Andor had not yet moved his army, but that too was something he needed to do--learn what he could of the enemy.

They spied the unwieldy army little more than a day's ride, by surface beast, from the Andor's royal palace. A little surprised to see that they had not yet even crossed the border of their own lands, Talin circled above them for a time, dropping lower and lower to better see what was going on.

They were camped. As it was in the middle of the day, Talin found that circumstance peculiar. He could think of no reason for it save that they were waiting for others to arrive. Climbing the air currents once more to a higher altitude, he considered the matter. Finally, summoning two of those he'd brought with him, he sent them to try to infiltrate the group gathered below, to see what they might learn from the talk of the soldiers.

Three others, he sent to scour the countryside for the soldiers they were no doubt waiting for, with instructions to meet him at King Andor's palace once they had gathered whatever information they could.

The castle was closed up tightly, which he had expected. It was also well defended, which he had also anticipated.

He hadn't entirely foreseen the ferocity with which the defenders seemed determined to guard their king's holdings. The moment he and his men began to circle lower toward the battlements, they encountered a hail of arrows and spears. Withdrawing to a little safer distance, he considered the situation and finally instructed his men to gather stones for a bombardment.

It had the desired effect of driving the soldiers inside, but the moment he and his men ran out of stones to drop, the man children rushed back onto the battlements and commenced to lobbing spears and arrows once more.

He was a little disconcerted to discover the task he'd set for himself was proving to be a bit more difficult than he'd expected. There was nothing for it, he finally decided. They were simply going to have to accept that they could not crack this nut without a few casualties.

The only alternative that he could see was to draw them out until they'd exhausted their supply of weapons, and he had a feeling that would take longer than he was willing to devote to the project.

Withdrawing again, he waited until the three he'd sent off to reconnoiter joined the fray. Taking three men with him, he set the others the task of a relay bombardment with stones to keep the defenders occupied while he and the others breached the lines to gather what they'd come for.

As he'd hoped, most of the soldiers had gathered to defend the side of the castle under attack. Nevertheless, they did not manage to gain the roof top garden without detection. A fairly determined assault was launched by the men still guarding the other side of the castle. He, himself, had a narrow miss, and one of the men took a direct hit, an arrow piercing one thigh.

The most dangerous time, however, came once they had landed, for they needed to shift in order to complete their goal. The wounded man, slowed by his injury, caught yet another arrow as they settled in the garden, this one in the chest.

He was too wounded to shift. In his current condition he needed to remain in his beast form to heal or he would die. By the time they'd managed to drag him to shelter, all of them were wounded and bleeding.

Talin's own wound was fairly superficial. An arrow had grazed his throat, but it closed almost at once and the blood ceased to flow down his shoulder and chest.

Leaving his men to remove the arrows they'd caught so that their wounds could close, he headed toward the door that let out into the garden.

It was a stout door, and well fortified from what he recalled of his first visit to the palace. His memory served him. It was heavily barricaded. Using his shoulder as a battering ram, it still took three heavy hits before the wood splintered and the heavy timber bar on the inside split. Summoning his men, he shoved the broken door out of the way. The only warning he got that the corridor was manned was the whistle of an arrow. It embedded itself into a fragment of door next to his shoulder. Wrenching what was left of the door from the hinges, he used the stout wood as a shield and rushed the men crowded at the top of the stairs on the opposite end of the corridor. Those at the top fell back before his assault, creating a domino effect and bringing down the men behind them.

Tossing the shield after them, he whirled and raced back the way he'd come to the only interior door that opened off that particular corridor and slammed a shoulder against the panel. The interior door wasn't nearly as stout as the exterior one. It caved in with the first blow and his impetus took him inside to a chorus of feminine screams and a barrage of missiles that included everything from pillows to pitchers, bowls, vases and even a small chest.

"Cease!" he roared when he'd tired of batting the missiles and dodging them.

. They stopped, but he thought that was more because they'd run out of anything to throw than because of the bellowed order. 'Weaponless' now, the half dozen women in the room scurried to the farthest corner to cower in fear as his men dashed inside behind him. After looking around a little wildly, the men dashed across the room and grabbed a large armoire, carried it back to the now splintered door and covered the opening before the castle defenders could regroup and launch another attack.

"I've come to gather the princess' belongings," Talin announced, planting his hands on his hips and fixing the women with a stern stare. "Make haste and gather her most prized possessions."

The women merely gaped at him as if he'd spoken to them in a foreign language.

"Now!" he bellowed.

The yell evoked another chorus of shrieks, but the women only covered their ears, hid their faces, and crowded a little more tightly together. Uttering a growl of impatience, Talin stalked across the room and looked them over. The one with the dark mahogany hair looked vaguely familiar, as did the one with pale blond hair. Grabbing the first, he hauled her to her feet. "Your lady has need of you. Will you do nothing but cower in the corner like a frightened rabbit?"

The woman stared at him in horror. "She's ... she is alive?"

Talin glared at the woman. "Why would she not be?" he demanded.

Her jaw sagged in surprise, but after a moment, instead of responding verbally, she merely nodded jerkily and looked around the room blankly. Grabbing the satchel he'd brought to fill, Talin removed the long strap slung around his neck and over one shoulder and handed it to her. "Fill it--clothing."

He grabbed the blond and hauled her upright. Catching a second satchel one of his men tossed to him, he pushed it into the second woman's hands. "The princess' favored things."

When he'd dragged two more of the cowering women from the huddle and put them to work, he moved to the window to survey the lay of the land. Below, he could see the castle's defenders pouring into the palace from every direction. "We are about to have company," he muttered grimly.

Nodding, his men began to pile everything of weight against the barricade they'd created with the armoire. When they'd finished, most of the room's contents were piled in front of the door.

Commanding the women to hurry and finish, he moved to the window again and uttered the keening cry to call his men to arms. When he saw the first arrive to begin the bombardment of the palace, he turned to study the women again. He'd hoped to bring them all, but he had only three men with him and all of them were weakened from wounds. Disgusted that his plan had degenerated into a scramble to grab whatever could be taken quickly and certain that he would find when he returned that the mindless females hadn't packed the half of what they should have, he nevertheless realized that they had to go if they had any chance of carrying off what they'd gathered.

The two maids he'd first drawn from the group were the same two who had tried to defend Princess Aliya from him, and he felt certain the bond between them was strong. She would be most pleased, he decided if he took those two.

Unfortunately, the soldiers did not seem to care where they placed their arrows so long as they hit something. If he was not careful, he would end up delivering two corpses so full of arrows they looked like pincushions.

Striding to the bed, he began tearing strips from the linen.

Grabbing the blond, he bound her wrists together and shoved her toward the man least injured. "Carry her on your back where she will be protected," he said grimly.

Instantly, the woman began to scream and struggle.

Wincing at the high pitched shrieks, Talin tore another strip from the bedding and gagged her. They would all be deaf if they had to listen too much of that, to say nothing of the danger inherent in it. For it would not only make it impossible for him and his men to hear what they needed to hear, but would insure that everyone for miles around knew their exact position.

Almost as an after thought, when he remembered how terrified Aliya had been of the height, he tied a second strip over her eyes. Satisfied, he lifted her up and hooked her arms over his man's head and then turned and eyed the red head. The moment his gaze fell upon her she began to scream, dashing round and round the room in a blind panic.

The noise from the bombardment didn't help, nor the battering against the barricade.

Instead of chasing her around the room, he waited until she'd made the circuit and grabbed her before she could whirl and dart off in the opposite direction. The moment he seized her, she whirled on him and, curling her fingers into claws, went for his eyes. He caught her wrists, but he discovered he couldn't hold both and bind them. Gritting his teeth, resisting the urge to simply knock her out, he hunched one shoulder and ignored her pounding while he bound one wrist and then caught the one she'd been using to club him and tied that to the first. The gag came next, more because she'd resorted to trying to bite him than the screaming.

The barricade had begun to give way to the pounding from the corridor by the time he lined his men up at the window to depart.

It was too narrow to allow them to shift *before* they went out. They had, perforce, to dive from the window and shift as they fell. Despite the gags, both women screamed deafeningly as they plunged downward. He wasn't certain at what point the woman he was carrying lost consciousness, but he was in trouble himself by then and had little time to worry about it.

He was the last to leap from the window, and even as he shifted he felt a blazing hot poker pierce his chest that almost made him black out. At almost the same instant, two more arrows slammed into him, piercing his side and one thigh. Fighting to remain conscious and airborne, he managed to catch an updraft of wind and with that added buoyancy climbed beyond range of the archers.

The wounds were bleeding profusely. He knew that, knew also that they could not close so long as the arrows remained embedded in his flesh. He didn't dare land to see to the wounds, however. In his weakened state, he was far too vulnerable and the lands were crawling with the man children gathering for war.

His men were in no better condition, but he encouraged them onward. The sooner they reached the palace, the better off they would all be. Catching first one updraft and then another, the group managed to gain enough altitude to glide most of the way which was a fortunate circumstance since they were all in a sorry state and the effort to stay aloft with their burdens only made the task more difficult.

Despite the nearly blinding pain, Talin felt his spirits lift when he spied his palace in the distance. He was almost home. Aliya was going to be beside herself with joy when she saw what he'd brought her.

Chapter Eleven

Aliya felt a stab of unease run through her when she heard a shout and looked up to see the sudden alertness of the men manning the walls of the castle. Listening intently to hear what had caught their attention, she heard a great whoosh of air. It almost seemed to reverberate, bouncing from the mountainside across the courtyard where she walked and pinging from wall to wall, a ricochet of sound rather than an object.

Stopping, she tried to discern the direction of the noise. When she found she couldn't, she moved away from the wall so that she could see the men atop it better.

To the man, they had turned to gaze to the south--where Anduloosa lay.

Her heart fluttered uncomfortably at the thought, but before she could even fully form the hope that sprang in her mind, a tremendous golden falcon burst into view. It circled, spiraling lower with each pass and finally landed. Frozen with fear at the sight of the great bird of prey, it was several moments before Aliya realized that shadows raced along the ground all around her. Instinctively, she looked up, discovering more of the giant falcons.

Too stunned to move or to flee in any direction, she merely stood stock still, watching as they settled. Several, she saw, were carrying great, bulging leather satchels. They arched their necks, allowing the packs to slide from their necks and drop to the ground.

Two others carried not only satchels, but human burdens. She stared at the two women that crumpled to the dirt where they'd been dropped in disbelief and horror. They were captives. That much was obvious--their wrists bound, gagged, blindfolded. They scarcely moved after they'd fallen, merely lay where the fell, moaning piteously.

Anger began to boil up through her fear. Without even realizing she had done so, she began moving toward the two women. As she drew nearer, her gaze traveling over them for signs of injury, a prickle of recognition dawned and then blossomed when she recognized the clothing they were wearing as dresses that belonged to Lady Beatrice and Lady Leesa. Abruptly, she caught her skirts, lifting them away from her feet as she broke into a run.

By the time she reached them tears of pure rage were rolling down her cheeks. Her ladies! Her dear friends, battered, manhandled, frightened out of their wits, were struggling blindly to crawl away from their tormenters.

Uttering a cry of fury, she focused on the falcon nearest Lady Leesa and flew at him in a rage, hammering at him with her fists. "You monster! You conscienceless devil! What have you done to them?"

The falcon wavered. Abruptly, its legs gave out and it settled to the dirt and then fell over on its side. Losing her balance, Aliya fell on top of it. Her surprise killed her rage instantly. Stunned, she struggled to her feet, her gaze drawn from the great falcon to her hands by bright red blood. She stared at the blood for several moments and then down at her dress, feeling a wave of dizziness wash over her when she saw she was covered in blood.

Glancing from her dress to the bird, she saw that there were arrows protruding from his chest, his side, and one thigh. As she watched, he caught the shaft jutting from his chest with his beak and wrenched it free. Fresh blood gushed from the open wound.

She uttered a pained cry, feeling almost as if the arrow had been pulled from her own flesh. "Talin! By the mercy of the gods, what has happened?"

She was almost more stunned when he spoke to her in Talin's voice than she had been by anything that had happened before.

"Your father's archers send their greetings," he muttered, catching the second shaft and tearing that from his flesh.

Aliya clapped a hand over her mouth, feeling bile rush into her throat, though she wasn't certain what sickened her more, the ripping of his flesh, or the thought that her father had ordered this. "Don't! Please don't! You're only hurting yourself worse!" she cried as he caught the last arrow and tore it free.

Bursting into tears, she rushed to his head as he collapsed limply on the ground. Falling to her knees, she lifted his head gently and settled it in her lap, stroking his beautifully feathered face soothingly. "You are wounded nigh unto death! Why would you do such a thing?"

"I thought that it would please you," he muttered.

Uttering a sob, she grabbed a handful of her skirt, balled it and pressed it against the wound in his chest. "You fool!" she sobbed. "It doesn't please me at all to have you dead!" Bending over him, she lay her cheek against his, wishing she could think of something to do for him.

The chest wound, she knew, would be fatal. If it had only been the arrows in his side and thigh, he might have had some chance.

She wasn't certain of how long she lay like that, sobbing against his neck, but she finally became aware that he'd gone perfectly still. Lifting her head, she brushed the tears from her eyes with the back on one hand. His golden eyes opened, gazing up at her keenly.

It took all she could do to keep from bursting into tears again. He was too weak even to shift into man form again.

She covered her mouth when he closed them, certain that he was dying right before her eyes, that he would breathe his last. Instead, as she watched, he began to change before her eyes, his body shifting. At first, thinking that he was convulsing, a hot then cold flash of fear went through her. As she sat trying to blink the tears from her eyes, though, she saw his beak and feathers vanish, and then his head and body contort and change shape. Within moments, Talin, the man beast lay in her lap.

It was almost more frightening that he had shifted. Did they change to human form when they died, she wondered? Or had he used the last of his strength to change because he knew she felt only revulsion for the man beasts and he wanted her to see him as a man?

She didn't know, but he still breathed and she became abruptly determined to do whatever she could for him to make him comfortable. When she looked around for help, she discovered that everyone in the courtyard seemed frozen in a tableau of horror, unable to move.

Her ladies were no longer bound. Their gags and blindfolds had been removed, but they stood as still as statues behind her, their expressions bewildered, as if they weren't completely certain they were awake and not dreaming.

"Help me with him!" she said commandingly.

Both of them blinked, as if coming out of a trance, but neither moved. Before she could leap to her feet and slap them to bring them out of it, several men rushed forward. Grabbing Talin, they lifted him from the ground. Dismissing her maids abruptly, Aliya hurried to follow them as they moved Talin into the palace. "Be careful with him!" she said sharply. "He will begin to bleed again if you jostle him!"

In truth, she didn't think that he had ceased to bleed, but it would certainly not help at all for him to be battered and jostled by his men. The procession had reached the king's suite before she realized her ladies had followed, as docilely as puppies. "Find something that I can use to bind his wounds!" she snapped at them, rushing to grab the basin and fill it with water. "If only I had my medicines," she muttered.

"I brought the chest," Lady Leesa responded hesitantly.

Aliya glanced at her. "Then find it, and be quick about it!"

Without even glancing at the men who'd brought Talin up, settled him on the bed, and stripped his tunic off, she made a shooing motion in their general direction as soon as she'd settled the basin on the floor. He was conscious, she saw as she wet a cloth and began to carefully bathe the blood from his chest. Trying not to think of the pain he must be in, she focused on bathing the blood off until she could see the wound. Relief so profound it made a hard, painful knot in her throat went through her when she was finally able to see the wound. Instead of the great, deep hole she'd expected to find, she saw that it was not at all deep, a good deal more than a flesh wound, to be sure, but she could see that the arrow head had not penetrated beyond the muscle tissue.

Sniffing, she flicked a relieved glance at his face. "It is not nearly as bad as I had feared," she said reassuringly. "You will live."

Something flickered in his eyes when she spoke to him, but his expression was bemused. Smiling, she stroked his cheek reassuringly. "Really! It is not bad. I have herbs that will help to keep infection away … and more for fever if needed. In a few days, you will be fine. I am certain of it."

She wasn't, though. The herbs helped, but they did not always keep wounds from becoming infected. As often as not, the wounded survived the wound but died of the fever that came later.

Vaguely aware of a commotion behind her, Aliya dragged her attention from Talin to see what was going on. Several men had trooped into the room with the satchels she'd seen the golden falcons carrying. As they dropped them onto the floor and turned to leave, Lady Leesa and Lady Beatrice hurried to the packs and opened them, disgorging the contents all over the floor.

Recognizing her belongings, Aliya glanced at Talin again. "You risked your life for ... things?" she asked with a mixture of remorse and disbelief, remembering with shame the things she'd screamed at him when she'd seen her friends so roughly treated, remembering that she'd flown at him and tried to pound him to death with her fists.

He shook his head slowly. "So that you would not miss your home so much."

Aliya felt her chin wobble. Resolutely, she clamped her lips firmly together and rinsed the cloth again. The water, she saw, was red with blood. Setting the cloth aside, she went to the chamber pot to empty it and returned for fresh water from the pitcher.

"We will attend him," Lady Leesa said, rushing to the bed as Aliya reached it once more.

Aliya studied her friend for a moment. "No," she said finally. "I will see to his hurts. He was hurt because of me."

"Your grace! He is the next thing to naked," she whispered.

A faint smile curled Aliya's lips. "I have seen him completely naked," she whispered back. "I will not faint."

"It is not ... fitting for a maiden to tend a man--especially not a future queen," Lady Beatrice exclaimed in a hissing whisper.

Anger surged through Aliya. Why, she wondered, had she never noticed what snobs they were? "I will never be a queen now. I am King Talin's concubine."

Both women gaped at her in horror. "He ... he *dared* to ... to ravish *you*? And you mean to tend his hurts? You should leave him to die! Or better yet, slit his throat while he is weak."

It was only with a great effort of will that Aliya refrained from slapping Lady Beatrice at her cold, unfeeling comment. "Beyond taking me from my home, he has not *forced* me to do anything!" she snapped angrily. "And that is probably more than could be said of those who had come to fight over me … as if I was a bone and they dogs to snarl over my carcass! Do you think any one of them would have hesitated at all to claim me, willing or not, once I had been given into their keeping?"

Both of her ladies fell back as if she'd slapped them, staring at her as if they had never seen her before.

Perhaps she *was* a stranger to them, she thought wryly. Maybe they had never really known her at all. "You can make yourself useful by putting away my things," she said tightly, dismissing them abruptly and returning her attention to Talin.

He was watching her intently, she saw. Ignoring the questioning look in his eyes, she picked apart the tie that held up his loincloth and tossed it, almost defiantly, in the general direction of her ladies, who had moved to kneel beside one of the satchels. It smacked Lady Beatrice in the back of the head.

Biting her lip to keep from smiling, Aliya opened her chest of medicines and packed the wound she'd cleaned, folded a pad over it carefully and wrapped a strip of linen around his chest to hold it in place.

"Why did you bind them?" she asked abruptly.

He was silent so long, she glanced up, meeting his gaze. "To keep them from falling."

Guilt flushed her cheeks with heat. She had immediately thought the worst of him when she really had no reason to, she realized. She had been his prisoner for almost a week, and except for the rough beginning, which she had come to believe truly had been a misunderstanding, he had behaved surprisingly well. True, he had taken liberties he should not have, but she felt fairly certain that any of the men who'd vied for her hand in marriage would not have shown even that much restraint if she had been at their mercy.

She began to wonder why he had not claimed her body.

He seemed to desire her.

Was she wrong in believing that?

"And the blindfolds?" she asked after examining the wound in his side, just above his waist and finding that it, too, was no more than a shallow wound. He must have been nearly out of range when he had been hit she decided as she set about packing herbs in the gash and carefully bandaging that wound as well.

"To keep them from being frightened of the height."

She sent him a suspicious glance, but she could see nothing to indicate he spoke less than the truth. "I suppose the gags were also to protect them?" she asked dryly.

A faint smile curled his lips. "Those were to protect me."

A chuckle escaped her before she could prevent it. She shook her head as she finished binding the second wound and shifted to examine his thigh, trying hard to keep her gaze from straying to his genitals.

She found that impossible though she took care to examine his man root surreptitiously as she cleaned his thigh. It looked soft and she wondered at that, for she had been certain when he had lain upon her that it had been hard, and bigger than it appeared now.

Maybe that had just been her imagination, though, because she had been unnerved by the notion of him pushing it inside of her to lay his seed at her womb?

The thought alone was enough to bring a flush of awareness to her body, to make her belly clench, as if it was eager to grasp his manhood. Her hands trembled as she tended the wound and finally, to her relief, finished bandaging it.

"Why did you tell them you were my concubine?" he asked curiously, when she would have risen and moved away.

Embarrassed that he'd overheard, she focused on closing up her chest of medicines. "You said that you would claim me as your concubine," she said evasively.

"You allowed them to think I already had, though."

For a moment, she met his gaze. She found she couldn't sustain it, however. "They believed you had. I could see that." She thought it over for a moment. "Even if I could somehow go back now, no one would believe I was still a maiden."

Talin shifted, frowning. Thinking his wounds must be causing him pain, Aliya set her medicine chest on the floor and settled beside him on the bed, smoothing his hair from his cheek and stroking it soothingly. "I ... feel so badly that you were hurt trying to please me."

"Don't," Talin said harshly, grasping her hand and placing a kiss in her palm. "It is not your fault. None of the things that have happened are your fault."

Aliya sighed dejectedly, but made no attempt to retrieve her hand. "I fear that it is, or at least that I have become the pawn that everyone had been seeking for many years. It is because of me that they have found an excuse to make war."

Chapter Twelve

Acutely aware of the subdued voices of the women across the room, Talin lay staring up at the ceiling with a mixture of a dread, irritation, and more than a touch of resentment that he had, all unwittingly, found himself in an untenable situation.

The unpalatable truth was that he'd gotten himself into a hell of a mess and could think of no way to dig himself out of the hole.

Aliya was going to want to slit his throat when she figured it out, and she was bound to realize her mistake before much longer.

Grinding his teeth, he turned over, putting his back to the women. The moment he did so, he heard Aliya's quick step as she rushed over to the bed. Her hands settled on his shoulder and waist. "You mustn't move around!" she said chidingly. "You're liable to reopen the wounds."

Squeezing his eyes closed in vexation, he rolled onto his back again.

"Poor darling," Aliya said soothingly, stroking his cheek. "Are you in very much pain?"

"No," he said through gritted teeth.

"I should give you some herbs for the pain."

That was all he needed! To have his wits addled by some drug when he was already in a hell of a fix and couldn't figure a way out. "No!" he said harshly.

A look of hurt crossed her features, but after touching a hand to his forehead, she finally returned to her seat on the opposite side of the room.

He was going to go mad, he thought angrily. He wasn't certain which was worse, being confined to bed when there was nothing wrong with him, or having to endure being constantly stroked and petted--and aroused. It took all he could do to refrain from snarling at her to keep her hands to herself before he did something they would both regret.

Damn it to hell! He thought, disgusted all the way around with the situation. He'd been so blinded and mindless with pain by the time he'd landed in the exercise yard, however, he'd hardly known what he was doing. Except for his stunned dismay that Aliya, far from expressing joy at the gift he'd nearly died trying to bring her, had instead pounded on his pain wracked body until he'd thought he would pass out. He couldn't remember anything else very clearly. It had almost taken the very last of his strength to pull the arrows from himself so that his wounds could close and he'd been the next thing to unconscious when she'd begun to weep over him and carry on as if he was dying.

He had, in fact, wondered for several unnerving minutes if she knew something he didn't.

It had been stupid to squander so much of his little remaining strength to shift, particularly since he healed far faster in his beast form, but he had not been thinking clearly at all. All he'd been able to think about, in fact, was that Aliya was repulsed by his beast form.

And she was crying over him as if she was devastated to think he might die.

Which had moved him to nearly make it so by shifting before his wounds had even completely closed. He wasn't particularly worried about it. He felt stronger now, sore, but certainly well enough to be up and about his business. He could shift if he felt the need to make his body heal faster.

He would have shifted back, because he *was* in pain and he was still far weaker than he liked, except for one thing.

In the interim, between collapsing in the dirt and being carried to his bed, he had finally tumbled to the fact that Aliya was thinking of him as a man child, as if he was as fragile as her own kind was. By the time he'd come to his senses enough to figure that out, unfortunately, things had gotten way out of hand.

More awkward still he couldn't even put it all down to his weakness of the moment, not unless he included a weakness of the mind, because he had been well aware something wasn't quite right. He was just enjoying having Aliya taking on over him so much that he hadn't considered reassuring her that she had no reason to be so upset or fearful for him.

What the hell was he supposed to do now, he wondered? He knew damned little about the man children--except that they were weak. The simplest wound could kill them. Was a day long enough for recovery? Two?

He was going to be mad if he had to remain tied to the bed by his inadvertent lies for more than a day or two, especially if Aliya was determined to fondle him every time she came over to check his condition.

Aroused, was what he was, damn it to hell! Which she was bound to figure out the next time she decided to check his wounded thigh.

The alternative was to admit that his life was not in danger, but he discovered that he was almost as reluctant to face the rage that would entail as he was to give up the tender care Aliya seemed inclined to lavish upon him.

And the worst of it was that the longer he perpetuated her misconception of the situation, the more enraged she was likely to be once she found out.

For that matter, he didn't at all care for the deadly glances the two she-cats he'd brought Aliya kept sending his way whenever they thought Aliya wouldn't notice. If Aliya did lose her temper, she would have plenty of willing help to slit his throat and that was not the sort of wound even a man beast recovered from very often.

Not that he was particularly worried that they could manage it. He was weak, but not that weak. He was more concerned about the consequences of having to fight them off. As furious as Aliya had been about him binding them, she was not going to take it well if he had to forcefully subdue them.

Toward sunset someone tapped on the door. When Lady Beatrice answered it, his captain, Solly, poked his head around the door and peered toward the bed. Relieved at the distraction, Talin struggled upright, motioning for the man to approach him. The moment he did so, Aliya was out of her chair like a shot, pressing him back against the pillows. "You must be still and rest," she said chidingly.

Grimacing at her in a parody of a smile, Talin reluctantly settled back against the pillows, giving Solly a stern look and shaking his head ever so slightly. When she'd moved away finally and sat in her chair again, Solly looked Talin over questioningly. "I ... uh ... beg pardon for disturbing you, Sire, but I had news and felt that it could not wait."

"What?" Talin whispered harshly, abruptly completely focused on his captain.

"The men you sent to spy upon the man children have not returned."

Talin frowned, trying to calculate how much time had passed. "It may be nothing more than that they are finding it difficult to gather information," he said slowly. "But you were right to come. They are generally dependable?"

Solly nodded. "Two of my best, Sire. I can not be easy that they have not returned."

"If they have not returned by morning, I will go myself," he said finally.

Solly's brows rose. "Are you fit?"

Talin glared at the man, but he could feel his face reddening. "Well enough," he said firmly.

"Still, if you will forgive me, Sire, there is no reason why you should take such a risk, and every reason why you should not. You are weakened from your wounds, and you are needed by your people. I will go myself."

"I am not weak," Talin ground out in a hissing whisper.

Surprise flickered over Solly's features. "Then why are you abed?" he whispered back.

Talin felt his face darken with color again. "It is hard to explain," he said testily.

Solly stared at him for several moments. Finally, an unholy grin split his usually somber features. "It is because of your lady?" he asked intuitively.

"I am glad you find this so humorous," Talin snarled at him.

The smile vanished instantly, but Solly's eyes still gleamed with suppressed laughter. "She will be outdone when she discovers you have no lasting hurt," he said hesitantly.

"You think?" Talin growled irritably. "But that puts me in mind--give me your blade. Carefully, mind you."

Solly looked startled. "You think you will have need of it?"

Talin glanced away uncomfortably. "My wounds have closed. She will think that odd when she decides to change the bandages."

Solly's jaw dropped. "She will try to saw your head off with the thing if she discovers your deception."

"What do you suggest then?" Talin demanded testily.

"If I may be blunt?"

"You have been nothing else that I have seen!"

"Confess and beg forgiveness for not being near death," Solly responded promptly, his grin returning. "Else you might live to regret it."

Shrugging when Talin merely glared at him, he leaned down closer, allowing Talin to slip his blade from its sheath and tuck it beneath the pillow. "I am not that anxious to have her looking upon me again as if I am some sort of monster," Talin muttered.

Uneasiness went through him when Aliya rose and followed Solly to the door, speaking to him in a low voice. Nodding, Solly sent him an amused glance and left.

He watched her intently as she returned to the chair, wondering what they had discussed, resisting the urge to summon her and demand to be told. For perhaps thirty minutes, he stewed over it. Finally, the door opened and two maids trooped inside. One carried a tray upon which sat a bowl.

His stomach instantly clenched with hunger.

Aliya and her ladies rose from where they'd been seated. Her two ladies followed the other maid out of the room. Aliya, after glancing around as if looking for something, grabbed the edge of one of the smaller tables and dragged it to the side of the bed nearest him. The surprised maid followed her with the tray.

Taking it, Aliya smiled at her and waved her away.

Talin struggled up on one elbow to see what the bowl held.

"It's gruel," Aliya said in answer to the look on his face. "You lost a great deal of blood. This will help you in your recovery."

"I would far rather have real food," Talin retorted sullenly.

She smiled. "You must already be on the mend to be so cross."

He sent her a quick glance. "I am. I want real food."

"Tomorrow--if you're feeling better," she said chidingly, reaching for the pillow beside him and tucking it beneath his head.

Grinding his teeth, Talin sat glaring at her petulantly while she spoon fed him the noxious, thick broth, grimacing with distaste every time he swallowed.

"I am still hungry," he complained when he had managed to drain the bowl.

She looked at him in surprise. "I can send for more," she said hesitantly.

Immediately feeling faintly ill, Talin shook his head, settled back on the pillows, and draped an arm across his eyes, trying to get his mind off of his stomach, which alternately growled, demanding real food, and sloshed with the liquid she'd already poured down him.

As far as he could see the unpleasant side of this invalid business was rapidly beginning to outweigh any advantages. True, Aliya seemed to have not only lost all fear of him, but even to enjoy caressing him affectionately, but that was almost the worst of it. If he truly had been ill and weak, he might not have noticed. As it was, his mind told him it was merely to soothe, and his body told him something else entirely.

There must be *some* way to escape this tangle unscathed, he thought irritably, wracking his brain for an answer and coming up empty … again.

"You have sent your maids away," he said, more because he was bored stiff than because he had any real interest in where they'd gone or why.

"They were still very frightened," she said quietly, "and worn out from--everything that had happened. I thought it best if they went to rest. You should try to sleep."

Would that he could! He said nothing, though, because he was busy rehearsing possible scenarios in his mind for a confession that would free him from her tender clutches and still allow him to escape with his hide--and possibly his dignity--intact. He had always thought he was very nimble minded, but each time he tried to form some sort of explanation, he came up blank.

'I am feeling much better now' sounded like a promising beginning, but he had little hope that he could escape without saying more than that. 'It was only flesh wounds, barely a scratch' sounded even better to his mind until he recalled that she had examined him fairly thoroughly and stuffed those stinking herbs into the holes. Somehow, he didn't think he could convince her that she had been mistaken.

Jaide Fox

Into his jumbled thoughts, sounds intruded, quiet footsteps that were not Aliya's and the scrape of something on the floor. He ignored it, still pondering his dilemma, until he heard the distinctive splash of water. The moment he did, his mind instantly put the previous sound together with tub and bath.

For him? Or for her?

His cock had no preference. He instantly went hard. Lifting his arm fractionally, he blinked a couple of times to clear his vision and peered in the direction of the sound just in time to see Aliya step into the tub of steaming water. His throat closed, nearly strangling him as she lifted first one leg and then the other over the side, giving him a very good view of his heart's desire--his soldier's desire, anyway, for 'he' came instantly to full attention.

Shifting onto his side before she could notice the tent his soldier had erected, he lowered his arm fractionally.

She had gone as still as a statue, staring at him.

More than half expecting her to leap from the tub and race over to make him lie on his back again, he braced himself, trying to tamp the image that instantly leapt into his mind of grabbing her and tossing her on to the bed on her back. Mildly disappointed when she didn't, he nevertheless relaxed fractionally, trying to control his breathing before she realized he wasn't asleep and decided *not* to give him the show he hoped for.

When he heard the trickle of water again, he opened his eyes a fraction.

Apparently, she'd decided he was asleep, but she looked nervous and she bathed quickly instead of lingering as he had hoped.

Even so, he was in pure torment by the time she climbed out of the tub, dried herself off and pulled a gown over her head. The gown, he discovered, didn't help. His mind was filled with the image of her nakedness and it refused to be banished.

When he'd lain on his side until he was in agony from the blood still pounding through his veins, tightening his testicles until they felt like they were in vice, and engorging his manhood, he decided he had feigned sleep as long as he could stand it and rolled over onto his other side, putting his back to her. It was some relief. Not much, but some, for he managed to regain a modicum of control and ceased to feel like he was suffering the torments of the damned.

He didn't realize he'd been muttering curses beneath his breath until she appeared at the bedside and leaned over him. He nearly jumped out of his skin when she laid a cool hand on his brow.

"You are hot," she murmured, more to herself, he thought, than to him.

He was, but he doubted she would be willing to give him what he needed to cool down. The water from the tub, maybe, he amended, but not what he needed.

"You do not feel so feverish as to be delirious, though," she added thoughtfully.

He *was* delirious, he thought indignantly, and if she didn't stop stroking him she was going to find out just how far gone he was!

He relaxed when she moved away again listening as the maids cleaned up from her bath and finally left. The creak of the chair told him Aliya had returned to sit in the chair. Abruptly, he rolled onto his back and sat up. "You do not mean to try to sleep in that chair?"

He'd hardly gotten the words out when she'd leapt to her feet to rush over to him. "You must not be moving about like this!" she scolded, pushing against his shoulders and trying to make him lie down again. "If you reopen those wounds, we shall both be very sorry. Try to sleep."

He was sorry now. "I can not sleep if you mean to sit across the room all night and stare at me," he muttered irritably.

She settled on the bed beside him, smoothing his hair. "I do not like the thought of leaving you alone. What if you should need something?"

He was about to snap at her again when a thought occurred to him. "I would rest better if I knew you were resting," he said with cunning.

She looked a little self conscious at the suggestion. "I might disturb you."

"You wouldn't," he responded earnestly.

She considered it for several moments while he held his breath. "All right. I *am* tired," she confessed. "But you must tell me if I disturb you."

It took all he could do to keep from leering at her when she climbed into the bed beside him and lay down. Rolling onto his side to face her, he hooked a hand around her waist and dragged her close, burrowing his face against her neck and breathing in her fresh scent ecstatically.

"You should not do this," she said pushing at his shoulder. "You will cause yourself hurt."

"I am very comfortable as I am," he murmured in a strangled voice, settling more firmly against her.

She subsided after a moment, stroking his back in what he supposed was intended to soothe. Under other circumstances, he might have felt that way about it. At the moment, though, it was more like stoking the embers.

Tiring of merely smelling her skin, he nuzzled his way downward until he had planted his face between her breasts, trying to nudge the neck of her gown a little lower with his chin so that he could actually touch skin instead of the gown. She tensed slightly, but she didn't attempt to pull away. Deciding that must mean she was open to the idea, after a moment he wound his way up the hillside to the peak.

She hitched in a breath and held it before he even touched the taut bud of flesh and he felt a rush of heated desire at her response. Covering the tip with his mouth, he sucked it through the thin fabric, alternately toying with the sensitive flesh with his tongue and suckling until she began to move restlessly as if she could no longer hold still.

He found he couldn't either as the fire of need poured through him. Shifting so that he was supporting most of his weight on his side and one arm, without releasing the prize he'd already captured, he slipped his free arm upward and cupped her other breast, massaging the soft globe.

A soft moan escaped her, driving him over the edge of reason. Shifting again, he thrust against her hip and thigh, almost groaning at the bursts of pleasure the pressure against his cock sent through him with each arch of his hips. In a mindless search for more, he released the breast he'd been massaging and skimmed his palm down her body to her hip, and then her thigh, grasping a handful of her nightgown and slowly gathering it into his hand.

"Talin," she whispered a little shakily. "You should not do this."

She sounded as if she wasn't completely convinced he shouldn't, so he decided to ignore the warning. Shifting over her, he released his grip on her gown long enough to scoop her other breast from the neck of the nightgown and sucked the other trembling peak into his mouth. This time, he touched only flesh, tasted her. He groaned at her sweet taste. His heart pounded with bruising pressure against his ribs. She uttered a choked gasp as he began to suckle and tease it as he had the first. The sound sent him deeper into madness and pushed reason far to the back of his mind.

Grasping the gown he'd bunched around her hips, he yanked it higher and slipped his hand beneath to caress her belly, hips, and thighs, moving a little closer and a little closer to his ultimate goal when she allowed his caresses without protest.

Chapter Thirteen

Aliya was scarcely aware of the mesmerizing caress of his hands. Her entire being seemed focused inward, gathering pleasurable sensations into a collective like drops of rain into a pool of water--or, perhaps more accurately, like molten lava into a fiery pool. She was hot, dizzy, and breathless. Her belly quaked, her woman's place inside quivering with want, growing hot and achy and damp.

She couldn't help but clench her inner muscles as he rubbed his hardness against her mound, stirring her in a way no maiden should want.

A sense of excitement and anticipation had gripped her the moment he began to suckle her nipple. Her breath grew short yet heavy, her heartbeat felt erratic. Her desire grew with tremendous, dizzying speed until she found herself reaching for the unspecified 'something' the building inside of her promised.

She was so deeply under its spell that she wasn't entirely certain of how his hand had found its way beneath her gown. She discovered she didn't care either. Warmth lit her skin every place he touched, warmth and pleasure.

He pinched her nipples with delightful pressure, massaged her breasts until she thought she would burst, and all the while her cleft grew moister.

Something nagged at her, though, something that kept intruding a note of warning into the web of delight he was weaving around her. The 'something' didn't coalesce in her mind, however, until he skimmed his palm across her belly and cupped his fingers over her mound.

He wanted to join with her, she realized abruptly.

Without kissing her lips even once, he had enthralled her, swept every consideration from her mind with the wondrous sensations he created with no more than the light stroke of his hand and his mouth.

She didn't want him to stop. She found that she was too far gone to fight the desire to continue, that he'd caught her off guard and unaware and stoked the fire inside of her until neediness outweighed any fears that might have lingered.

She felt a jolt go through her when his fingers dipped lower, sizzling along her nerve endings like lightning as he parted the tender flesh and rubbed his finger across a bud of flesh that was excruciatingly sensitive. Her clit pounded like a second heartbeat, becoming instantly rigid against his fingers as they slipped through her cleft.

Aliya gasped, arching her back, unwittingly bringing herself harder against his hand. He groaned, but she couldn't tell whether from pleasure or pain.

She shouldn't be doing this.

He shouldn't be doing this.

"Talin," she gasped a little desperately as her anxiety for him finally pierced the euphoria she seemed to be drowning in, "you will reopen your wounds. You could die."

"I would die happy," Talin muttered as he released the nipple he'd been teasing and plotted a sneak attack to silence her belated objections, nibbling kisses up her throat to capture her lips and then taking a detour to her ear.

"Do not say things like that!" she gasped shakily, grabbing his arm when he slipped his hand lower along her cleft and found the gateway to paradise. He teased the edges of her opening, making her jerk in pleasurable reaction. "I ... could not bear it if anything happened to you because of me."

He plucked at ear lobe teasingly. "I need you," he said hoarsely, "need this. I ache for you until it is a torment to me." Ceasing his exploration of her body abruptly, he grasped her hand and guided it to his own flesh, cupping her hand around his distended shaft.

She gasped, her eyes widening, but after a moment she explored him from root to tip and back again with curious fingers, finally cupping his testicles gently.

The pleasure was so intense he uttered a choked cry, grinding his teeth against it as his face contorted with a mixture of pain and pleasure.

She released him as abruptly as if she'd discovered she had fire in her hand. He caught her wrist before she could withdraw, guiding her hand back and curling her fingers around his cock.

"I need you," he murmured, burrowing his face along the side of her neck as he held her hand firmly against his flesh and rocked against her palm.

Aliya felt her heart squeeze with empathy at the pain she heard in his voice, the agony she saw on his face. Still, she hesitated, wondering if she would only cause him more pain if she allowed him what he wanted. The moment the thought of his wounds intruded, however, the tide turned in his favor. She found she couldn't bear the thought that he might die and leave her with the memory of his pleas for succor.

She wasn't sure if it was her own needs that prompted the thought, or merely the need to comfort him, but she caved in to it. "I am yours," she whispered shakily.

He tensed all over. Lifting his head to look down at her, he studied her face for a long moment and abruptly covered her mouth with a kiss of such ravening, possessive hunger that it almost instantly ousted the sense of willing sacrifice to his needs and replaced it with the burning need she'd felt before. The rake of his tongue along hers filled her with his taste and scent like strong liquor, devastating her senses in a dizzying rush of pleasure.

He slipped over her, pressing a knee between her thighs until she yielded to the pressure and parted them for him.

The moment she did, he pushed them wider still, settling his other leg beside the first and arching his pelvis into hers. His manhood pressed against her nether lips until they parted and she could feel his heated, engorged member caressing her damp, sensitive crevice.

It sent a shock wave through her that was a mixture of anticipation and fear.

Before her uneasiness could gain the upper hand, he broke the kiss and dipped downward, capturing the peak of her exposed breast between his teeth and bearing down until she gasped at the sharp needles of pleasure.

Catching the fabric at the neckline of her gown, he tugged at it until the fragile fabric parted and then moved to tease her other nipple.

Only dimly aware of anything beyond the sharp needles of pleasure that bombarded her senses with every hard pull of his mouth on the tender tip, Aliya responded mindlessly to his insistent tug on the back of her knees, drawing up first one and then the other. She could scarcely catch her breath, gasping hoarsely in her struggle to draw in enough breath and still feeling blackness press closer and closer.

The hard knot of flesh that was abruptly wedged into her womanhood, stretching it almost painfully sent a jolt of sudden awareness through her, however. She tensed all over, her eyes flying wide open as he pressed with slow but determined pressure. "Talin?" she gasped, her voice shaky now with fear as she abruptly recalled that every maiden she'd ever heard speak of this had complained of the pain.

He covered her mouth again, silencing her sudden attack of doubt with another fiery kiss, pressing into her relentlessly, easing away slightly, and then pushing forward again, delving deeper each time. Struggling to adjust to the alien intrusion, Aliya found she couldn't focus her mind away from it. Slowly but surely, discomfort was edging out the pleasure of before.

He stopped. Breathing like he was dying, he wrenched his mouth from hers and ran a shaky hand over her body, stroking her breasts, massaging them. Arching his back so that he could reach her breasts, he began to tease the tender nipples again, first one and then the other until heat rose in her as it had before, stronger than before and she began to sob with need.

He reached between their joined bodies after a moment, seeking the tiny nub of flesh that had created such need in her before and began to tease it. Aliya gasped at the sharp waves of sensation that raced through her, bucked his hand. In moments she found herself uttering hoarse cries that rose to a higher pitch as ecstasy abruptly burst inside of her. Even as her body quaked with the shock waves of rapture, he slipped his hand from her clit to her hips and thrust sharply, embedding himself deeply. A breaker of stinging pain ruptured the upsurge of pleasure as he withdrew slightly and plunged deeply again, leaping into a frantic, rhythmic pace, driving into her until she felt herself slipping upward, away from his pounding thrusts. She wrapped her arms around him tightly, bracing herself as he moved faster and faster and finally uttered a strangled cry, jerking and surging and washing her insides with the liquid heat of his seed.

A sense of triumph settled over Aliya when he went limp against her, sprawling bonelessly against her. It almost felt as if they were melding together in the heated aftermath of their lovemaking. It hadn't hurt nearly as much as she had feared it would. In fact, she had felt such pleasure before he'd taken her maiden head, she knew now why so many people were so obsessed with mating.

Her maiden's shroud was gone now and she was a woman.

Talin's woman.

The sense of warmth and belonging began to fade as discomfort began to set in from his heavy weight upon her, and then a touch of anxiety emerged, growing deeper as she came to her senses enough to remember he was an injured man.

She was slightly relieved when he finally gathered himself with an effort and rolled off of her, but she needed to reassure herself that he had not reopened his wounds. Raising up on one elbow as he collapsed weakly on his back beside her, she slipped her fingers beneath the wrapping that held his bandage in place and gently lifted one corner of the pad to see his wound.

A frown drew her brows together when she saw only pinkened, healing skin. Sitting up straighter, she pulled the pad all the way back and stared at his chest, feeling perfectly blank when all that met her gaze was new skin.

Talin, still struggling to catch his breath, tensed all over, meeting her dumbfounded gaze warily when she finally transferred her attention from his 'wound' to his face.

"There is a simple explanation," he said warily.

"How simple?" Aliya asked, anger already simmering in her voice.

"I heal quickly."

Aliya's eyes narrowed. "How quickly?"

"In beast form, almost at once--as long as there is nothing preventing the flesh from closing--more slowly when I shift to human form," he added quickly.

"You ... bastard!" she snarled, balling her hand into a fist menacingly. "You let me make a complete fool of myself, dashing around frantically to try to save your hide when you were in no danger any of the time!"

"That is not strictly true," he said defensively. "I was nigh dead when I first arrived in the courtyard. If I had waited much longer before I removed the arrows, I might well have died."

"So you were already healing even before I had you brought up to your 'death bed'?"

"I was weak, half crazy with the pain," he growled.

"Pain? I'll give you pain," she growled back at him, looking around for something to belt him with. "If I had a knife I'd put in your treacherous heart, you devil! You *tricked* me into giving myself to you!"

Suddenly keenly conscious of the dagger he had tucked beneath his pillow, Talin slipped his hand under the pillow and very carefully reached back until he could trust the dagger between the mattress and the ropes holding the bed frame together. "I distinctly recall that you said, I am yours!" he muttered tightly, feeling better once he was certain she wouldn't find the blade.

Abruptly, she planted her hands on his arm. Strengthened no doubt by her fury, she heaved him onto his side, and rolled him out of the bed. He was so stunned by the move he hit the floor before he could even think to try to catch himself. "Get out!" she screamed, hanging over the side of the bed to glare down at him as he struggled to get to his feet.

"This is *my* suite!" he shot back at her indignantly, planting his hand on his hips.

Uttering a growl of rage, she looked around for something to throw. Seeing her intent when she reached for the heavy candle holder on the table beside the bed, still filled with six fully lit candles, he whirled abruptly and stalked toward the door with as much dignity as he could muster.

The candle holder sailed past his head as he reached the door, narrowly missing him.

"Damn it to hell!" he yelped, whirling to face her. "You damned near hit me, you termagant!"

"I won't miss next time," she promised, scrambling out of the bed and heading for the water pitcher.

Deciding discretion was the better part of valor, he yanked the heavy door open and went out, slamming the stout panel behind him even as he heard the tinkle of shattering pottery. "Like it or not, you are still mine," he bellowed at the door.

The basin followed the pitcher, shattered on the door, and then joining the broken pieces on the floor.

He was half way down the tower stairs before the heat of his anger dissipated enough that it occurred on him he didn't have a stitch of clothing on. He stopped. Grinding his teeth, he glanced back toward the door of his suite, where his entire wardrobe was kept. Deciding that he wasn't particularly interested in rejoining the battle at the moment, he finally turned and continued down the stairs.

Silence fell as he stalked across the great hall and flung himself into his throne.

The seat, he discovered the moment his bare ass settled, felt like a sheet of ice and he almost came up off of it again.

A couple of the men gathered at one table in a game of chance uttered something that sounded suspiciously like a snicker and then fell into a fit of coughing when he sent a glare in their direction.

After brooding over the fickleness of women for some time, Talin lifted his head and surveyed the hall again until his eyes lit on a maid who was standing stock still, gaping at him. "Find me something to wear in the laundry," he bellowed at her.

She jumped all over, dropping the pitcher of ale she'd been holding. Nodding jerkily, she glanced down at the mess she'd made and then decided to leave it for the moment and hurried from the great hall.

"Sometimes they toss the clothing after," Solly said tentatively.

Talin sent him a narrow eyed glare at the man who'd intruded into his dark thoughts. "Then go and look," he snarled finally.

Hooking one leg over an armrest, he settled more comfortably, dropping an arm along the other rest and drumming his fingers on it impatiently while he waited. When Solly appeared again, he glanced at him questioningly.

Solly shook his head. "From the sound of it, I think she's building a barricade."

Talin frowned. "I do not understand women," he growled. "One moment, they are as sweet as honey, and the next they are threatening to cut your heart out."

"She did not find the dagger?" Solly asked uneasily.

"She had not when I left, else I would probably have it in my back now," Talin retorted. "She hurled everything else she could lay hand to at me. I confess, I had not thought she had such a temper. In general, she is so sweet, so gentle and loving."

Solly cleared his throat. "I did try to warn you, Sire, that she would not take the deception well."

Talin studied the man in fuming silence for several moments. Finally a morose expression replaced the anger. "I lost my head," he mumbled.

"Almost literally," Solly retorted, drawing another glare.

Since the maid arrived just then with the clothes he'd demanded, Talin decided to ignore that assault to his dignity. Grabbing the clothing, he sent the maid off to fetch him a tankard of ale to take the chill off. "And food. Real food!" he called after her as she took off again.

Standing, he ignored Solly's amused look and adjusted his loincloth. Apparently, it wasn't actually his, for he had some difficulty corralling his soldier and friends, who kept trying to escape whenever he moved. After a moment, he gave up the effort and grabbed the tunic she'd brought, looking it over suspiciously before he thrust his arms into it. This, too, he discovered, belonged to someone else, for he found he couldn't put his arms down once he'd managed to shrug into it. Uttering a growl of frustration, he flexed his arm and back muscles. The tunic split down the back, but he managed to get his arms down.

Disgusted when he saw he couldn't fasten the thing, he grabbed the breeches she'd brought and examined them. Those, at least, seemed to belong to him and he pulled them on and fastened them. "Any word from our spies?" he barked at Solly as he dropped into his seat once more.

His left testicle fell out in the process, strangling on the loincloth as it was pulled taut by his movements. Nausea washed over him. Grinding his teeth, he slipped a hand beneath his waistband, examined the injured one carefully and stuffed it back into the loincloth.

Solly's amusement vanished. He shook his head. "Nothing."

Glancing around the great hall, Talin discovered the carpenters had been busy. Most of the windows were covered by shutters. He caught a glimpse of moonlight, however, through one that still allowed a view of the sky. "I should not have sent them when we had no doubt already been spotted," he muttered, his anger turning inward. "But I had not thought, with so many new soldiers arriving, that two more would attract notice. The moon will set soon. We should go now when we can do so without attracting attention to ourselves and then disguise ourselves and enter the encampment in the morning."

"We?" Solly asked, alarmed. "Sire! You can not risk capture. The people need you."

"*I* need to know if the man children are of any real threat to us, and, if so, how great a threat," Talin retorted grimly.

Chapter Fourteen

His trunks, Talin discovered when he decided that Aliya had had long enough to recover her temper, had been dragged out into the corridor. After staring at them in surprise and dawning outrage for several moments, he stalked to the door. It was bolted, or still barricaded, from the inside.

He hammered on the door with his fist. "Aliya! This is childish. You are my concubine. You can not lock me out forever!"

He waited several moments. When he heard nothing, he pressed his ear to the door. Inside, he heard furtive movements that told him the room was indeed occupied. "You have defied your king *and* your husband, for you and I both know that you are well and truly mine! You may be sure that I will expect a full apology before I even *begin* to consider pleasuring you again!"

Something heavy struck the door even as he put his ear to it, certain the panel was just too thick to allow him to hear her. "You and I and now the entire palace!" she screamed at him furiously. "I could cheerfully *slay* you!"

His lips tightened. "They would have known anyway! We are man beasts. When a male has marked his female we sense these things, *know* them." He hesitated for a moment. "You said yourself that everyone believed as much already."

Another heavy object crashed into the door. Again there was no sound of shattering pottery or glass and he deduced that she had run out of light weight missiles of that nature. He waited for many moments, wondering if she would reconsider. He was angry enough to stalk away right then, but it had been *days* already. He was not going to be accountable for his actions if she continued to spurn him.

"Very well," he growled finally. "Soon I will go off to war. We will talk when I return. *If* I return," he added for full effect.

He heard brisk footsteps approaching the door on the other side and tensed, wondering if she meant to snatch it open and try to crack him over the head with something, or if the threat of death—his--had had the desired effect.

"If you go off and pick a fight with my father, I will never speak to you again as long as I live!"

That wasn't precisely the response he had expected and it took him several moments to realign his thoughts. "I did not start a war with your father! It is he who provoked this dispute."

"And you returned the insult by making me your whore!" she snapped. "You may go to him and say that I have accepted my fate and wish that he will make peace."

Talin ground his teeth, uncertain of which part of that speech infuriated him more. "You are my concubine!" he growled finally.

"It is the same thing."

"It is *not*!" he bellowed furiously. "I have had many laymen in my time, but I have not once taken a concubine! You are my first wife ... after the queen, which I have not taken," he added conscientiously.

She was silent for several moments. "I do not believe that even a king should have the right to take two wives," she ground out finally.

"It is our custom! And what is more, it is not only the king who does so!"

"It is not *my* custom. And I can not feel that I am bound only to one man, when he is not similarly bound."

For the first time since they'd begun the quarrel, Talin felt real fury grip him. "If you do not want the blood of many on your hands, do not even consider that as a possibility," he murmured, his voice almost deadly quiet now.

She was silent for so long that he thought she would say nothing else. Finally, she said, "Why should I worry about the blood of your people, when you mean to let the blood of my own?"

Uttering an impotent snarl, Talin whirled and stalked back down the tower stairs to the great hall.

Deciding she had been the victor in that round when she heard Talin stomp off, Aliya turned on her heel and rejoined her ladies. They sat in silence for some time, focused upon the needlework Lady Leesa had had the foresight to pack when she had been scrambling to gather Aliya's belongings. After some time had passed, Lady Beatrice uttered a snorting laugh. When she did, Lady Leesa let out a giggle.

Aliya sent them both a cross look. "I do not know what it is that you find so humorous," she said irritably.

Lady Beatrice shrugged, but after a moment uttered another snorting laugh. Again, Lady Leesa echoed it.

"What is it that you find so amusing?" Aliya demanded, beginning to be angry about the whole thing since she was still angry with Talin anyway.

And uneasy about the threat, for that matter, regardless of the fact that she'd challenged him over it.

"He will withhold his favors," Lady Beatrice muttered on a gurgle of laughter, whereupon Lady Leesa fell to laughing until tears began to flow down her cheeks.

Aliya managed a faint smile, but in truth she didn't find the threat particularly amusing. She felt a blush heat her skin in spite of all she could do, in fact, for she had found the threat rather distressing. It was not as if she felt that she could not live without his lovemaking, but he *had* pleasured her and she rather thought she would enjoy it even more the next time. Besides, in spite of everything, she had felt a wonderful sort of closeness afterward that she had liked almost as much as the other.

She *was* angry with him, and she not only felt that she had every right to be when he had deliberately deceived her to seduce her, she also felt that she was the one who deserved an apology.

Unfortunately, she had had time to discover that Talin was pigheaded. Now that he'd announced the threat to half the palace, he was going to be very reluctant to back down, even if he did come to accept that it was his fault and he should be the one to apologize.

She certainly wasn't going to, though it wasn't altogether because she felt that she was completely right and he was totally wrong. As difficult as it was to accept, she knew she had been guilty of bad behavior as well. Only a few moments ago he had provoked her until she had yelled at him and thrown things like a common fishwife instead of behaving with the dignity of her station.

He was an infuriating man! There was no doubt about it. He brought out the very worst sort of character flaws in her, faults she had not even been aware of having before.

She was not going to apologize for her own behavior, though, unless he apologized for provoking her to begin with.

She had a feeling that meant that there were going to be a lot of cold, lonely nights ahead for both of them.

* * * *

By the light of the setting moon, Talin and Solly left the palace, turning toward the valley where they had last seen the army of the man children. The moon had set long before they reached the location, but neither had any real need of the moonlight to see that the valley was now empty. Where before there had been many men, horses, cattle, wagons, tents--all the things the man children deemed necessary to make war--now there was only trampled grasses and mud from their passing.

After flying around the area in wider and wider circles for a time, they finally spotted the bulk of the army many miles east of their previous encampment. Leaving them for the moment, Talin and Solly struck off in search of the nearest hamlet and settled there, shifting into their man forms. When they'd managed to locate and 'borrow' clothing that would help them blend in, the left the village and found a place in a wooded area to spend the remainder of the night.

By sunrise, they were headed cross country toward the army. They emerged from the woodlands onto a narrow track before they came within sight of the encampment and followed that until they reached the spot where they had seen the army.

The encampment itself, they discovered to their surprise, had already been abandoned save for a handful of servants and guards. They had not even reached the guards, however, when the mystery was solved.

The army had moved off to engage an enemy.

Still puzzled since Talin had been under the impression that the army was marching on his own kingdom, Talin and Solly approached the guards to offer their services. After looking them over suspiciously for several moments, the guard finally addressed Talin. "You have experience in warfare?"

"Some. We are mercenaries."

"What engagements?"

Talin searched his mind for some of the battles fought in the past five years and claimed experience in a half dozen he thought were remote enough the likelihood of running into other participants was remote.

The guard frowned at him suspiciously. "I was at Medenhallow myself," he muttered finally.

Talin lifted his brows in surprise he didn't have to feign. "Were you fighting for King Mervin? Or King Anslar?" he asked.

"King Anslar."

Talin nodded. "We were fighting for King Mervin. One would think we would have met on the field."

The guard shrugged. "As to that, I suppose it would be unlikely given the size of the armies on both sides," he acknowledged grudgingly. "Well, as you can hear, you have missed the first battle, but we can use every man we can get. Find a place to bed down and be sure to speak to the pay master this evening."

Talin nodded. "Who is the enemy?"

The guard grinned. "Today? The clan of the wolf. When we have wiped those devils from the face of the land, then we will be marching once more."

Talin and Solly exchanged a speaking glance as they strode through the encampment. Once they were out of earshot of the guards, Solly spoke. "What do you make of that?"

Talin frowned. "Princess Aliya said something to me, but I will admit that I had my mind on other things and did not give it much credence anyway. She said that she feared she was being used as the excuse everyone had been looking for for many years."

"Excuse for what?" Solly asked in confusion. "To start a war with the clan of the wolf? I can not even see a connection."

Talin shook his head. "To begin a great war between the clans of the man children and the clans of the man beasts," he said grimly. "I had thought it odd that they had stopped to gather so far from my borders. Now it begins to make far more sense. They are certainly marching upon Goldone to make war, but they mean to do their best to wipe out every clan of the man beast between. And, if they succeed, they will turn from Goldone and march on the others."

Solly looked stunned. "Sire! You speak as if you think they have some chance of success."

Talin shrugged. "They have always outnumbered the man beasts, for they breed like rats, but I am certain there is something beyond their usual arrogance and the numbers they've mustered that makes them believe they can succeed, else they would not have launched such a campaign. I think, before we return to Goldone, we need to discover what has given them this sense of invincibility if we can."

Chapter Fifteen

Since they had no intention of remaining for any length of time, they did not follow the guard's advice and find a place to settle. Instead, they walked through the encampment and out the other side, following the sounds of battle.

The sun was high overhead by the time they finally reached the first signs of conflict. A man beast of the wolf clan lay dying amongst the bodies of his foes. Blood dripped from torn flesh, coated the ground liberally, and even dripped from the foliage of the trees and bushes nearby. Grim faced, Talin knelt beside the man.

"What means this?" he ground out, grasping the man beast's jaw and shaking him slightly when he saw the man was hardly aware of him. "Why have you not healed?"

With an obvious effort, the man beast focused upon him. "Can not," he managed to rasp hoarsely. "Poison."

Talin shook the man again as his eyes glazed, but he could not rouse him to speak again.

"Poison?" Solly echoed, dismay evident in his voice. "There is no poison to do such a thing."

Talin studied the dead man and then glanced around at the men he had killed before he had fallen. He saw nothing to explain the situation. It had been a vicious fight. To a man, including the man beast, all were torn and bloody from head to toe. "I am not at all certain the man knew what he was saying," Talin said slowly. "He was grievously wounded. Mayhap it is only that they attacked him so viciously, and dealt him so many wounds that he bled out before he could recover?"

Solly sent him a speaking glance. They both knew that that was unlikely, possible, but not probable.

Finally, without another word, they moved onward. The sounds of battle did not become louder as they progressed through the wooded area, although the signs that at least a part of the battle had taken place in and around the edge of the forest grew progressively more evident. They saw why when they finally emerged on a small knoll.

The battle had moved off beyond the smoldering ruins of what had once been the palace of the king of the clan of wolves but it was also obvious that the fighting, for the day at least, was mostly done. The dead and dying lay everywhere, crumpled, curled into fetal positions, sprawled bonelessly.

Among the man children were the man beasts--many of them.

Feeling vaguely ill, Talin glanced at Solly. Solly's expression was one of disbelief. "They are everywhere," he muttered. "The man children have slaughtered the clan of the wolf. I would not have believed this if I had not seen it myself."

For a time, they merely stood watching the battle still raging in the distance. Finally, Talin began to scan the full scope of destruction. On a rise to the west, he saw a group of men on horseback. One held the standard of the King of Anduloosa.

He struck off in that direction, picking his way around and over the fallen. Solly joined him after a few minutes. "It would be easier if we flew," Solly commented after a few moments.

"Mayhap," Talin said grimly, "but then they would be warned and would either flee to protect the king, or, more likely, attack, which would make it difficult to speak to King Andor."

"Sire! You will speak to him of peace over the bodies of so many man beasts, only because the princess demanded it?"

Talin sent him a furious glare. "I will speak to him of peace because my concubine asked it of me," he growled. "As sickening as this is, it has nothing to do with us. The clansmen of the wolf are not our brothers. But *he* is her father. She cares for him. If I can make peace for her sake, I will."

Solly frowned. "Do you think he will consider it?"

"No."

"Then I do not know why you would risk your life for a cause you know is lost before you even try. King Andor started the war by insulting us. I do not believe it was an oversight, whatever the princess thinks. I think it was very deliberate."

"It was. We were baited. They knew we would be too proud to ignore such a blatant insult."

"They?"

Talin glanced at his captain. "King Andor may or may not have devised this entire scheme on his own, but he is not alone in it. If they had gathered an army such as this, do you think it would have gone unchallenged? The neighboring kingdoms would have seen it as a threat and they would have moved to stop it before they amassed an army of this size. He used his daughter. By announcing far and wide that a tournament was to be held to settle her in marriage, he made certain that the heir of every kingdom had an excuse to gather that seemed unthreatening. And at the same time he saw to it that those who were deliberately slighted could not be unaware that they had been singled out for insult--the man beasts.

"He wants this war. He will not consider peace for the sake of his daughter, because he had intended to use her to make war from the beginning."

"If you are so certain of this, we should go. We should gather our army and prepare for war."

"We will, but first I will speak to him so that I can tell her daughter with a clear conscience that I tried."

"It is not worth your life!" Solly exclaimed. "Your people will need you."

Talin's lips curled faintly in a wry smile. "I do not intend to die."

"One never does."

By the time they had reached the foot of the hill the riders sat upon, they had been noticed. The men guarding the kings moved to block their path as they reached the summit. "You have no business here. Be gone!" one of the men growled when Talin and Solly had halted.

"I have come to speak with King Andor."

The man looked Talin over with obvious contempt. "Commoners do not address the king."

Talin barred Solly by extending his arm to block his path when Solly surged forward furiously. "It is as well then that I am not a commoner," he retorted.

King Andor nudged his horse forward. "You are brazen. What are you called?"

"My clansmen call me king."

Andor looked him over speculatively. "I do not know you," he said dismissively and began to turn away.

"I am husband to your daughter."

Andor stopped abruptly. Leaning over his pommel, he very deliberately spat, narrowly missing Talin's foot. "I have no daughter!" he growled.

Talin's face hardened with anger. "She will be devastated to hear that," he murmured menacingly. "She asked me to come to you and tell you that she has accepted … me and she wishes for you and I to make peace."

His face contorted with rage. "Accepted? No daughter of mine would *accept* a creature such as you, Talin. You are an abomination of nature. And I can not accept a whore of such as you as a daughter. She is dead to me. Would that she was dead in truth! It would be far better than what she has become!"

Talin's lips curled into a snarl. As quick as a snake strike, he shot upward, grasped the old man around the throat, and dragged him from his mount, shaking him. "Watch your mouth, old man! She is my concubine."

As stunned as they were by the swiftness of Talin's strike, the guards recovered quickly. A dozen spear tips bit into Talin's back, shoulder, and neck.

He ignored them. "Despite the insult to me and my clansmen, I have treated your daughter with the honor due her."

"Kidnapping her from her home? Raping her?" King Andor gasped gutturally past the hand squeezing his throat.

Talin gritted his teeth. "Do not confuse me with your own kind," he growled. "We do not take the unwilling or abuse the weak. She accepted me or I would never have touched her. It is only for her sake that I have come to offer peace."

"Keep your peace! And the whore! I want your blood!" King Andor snarled.

Talin's lips tightened. His hand tightened as well. "I could save myself a deal of trouble by throttling you now."

"It would stop nothing, save that you would return to my daughter with her father's blood on your hands. This war has been long in coming, but we are resolved. We will not stop until we have cleansed the land of the unnaturals."

"You have no daughter," Talin reminded him. "But I will give her your love. Call your dogs off." When King Andor merely glared at him, he shook the man.

After a lengthy pause, when Talin had begun to think the old man was willing to go to his death so long as he could take Talin with him, he sent the guards a commanding glance. The spear tips disappeared. When he saw that the guards had withdrawn a short distance, Talin glanced at his captain. "Go, Solly. Now!"

"Sire! I will not leave you!"

"Do as you are told!" Talin said commandingly

Saluting, Solly stepped back and commanded the transformation from man to falcon. As he spread his wings and leapt from the hillside, Talin grabbed King Andor's belt, lifted the man over his head, and tossed him toward the guards. He took off at a run while they were distracted by the flying man and their panicked horses, shifting as he ran and lifting off the ground and then struggling to climb into the air.

A spear whizzed past his head. A second one clipped the tip of one wing, but missed flesh. Solly, who'd wheeled in a tight circle, shot past Talin, heading directly toward the soldiers. When Talin had finally managed to gain enough altitude to be beyond range, he glanced around for Solly.

To his consternation, he saw that Solly was struggling. A spear had pierced his belly. Cursing under his breath, he turned and maneuvered until he could reach the shaft and wrench it free. He was on the point of dropping the spear, or launching it at the soldiers below, when an unpleasant thought intruded.

The man beast had said he had been poisoned. Twisting the spear so that he could study the tip, Talin examined it for anything that might indicate the presence of the poison the wolf had spoke of. He saw nothing on the spear, but when he turned to study Solly again, he saw that the wound had not closed. He was still bleeding profusely.

Trying to convince himself that that was a good thing, that if there was poison it could not enter Solly's body if the blood was washing it out, he focused on taking the most direct route to Goldone. He could see that Solly was growing weaker as they covered the miles between the kingdom that had once belonged to the clan of the wolf and Goldone. Relief flooded him when he at last spotted the palace in the distance.

"We are almost there, Solly."

"I do not think I can make it," Solly responded tiredly.

"Do not speak that way! I am your king! You will do as you are told!"

Solly rallied momentarily, but even as they approached the practice field in the center of the castle, Solly began to drop rapidly. Wheeling, Talin aligned his flight with Solly's and glided beneath him, nudging him upward.

"We will both fall to our deaths," Solly muttered.

"I have no intention of adorning the rocks below with my splattered carcass," Talin said grimly. "Or yours. Can you land?"

Solly gauged the distance. "Aye, Sire."

"You are certain?"

"Aye."

Talin dropped away. Satisfied when Solly managed to gain a little altitude, enough to clear the wall, he circled, watching as Solly descended on the other side. It was not a landing so much as it was a crash, however, and the moment Talin touched the ground, he dropped the spear he had carried, shifting to his man form as he rushed over to his captain to examine him. "The wound has not closed," he muttered. "Solly! Command your beast!"

"It is still there," Solly gasped hoarsely.

"It is not! I pulled the spear free!"

"I feel it," Solly groaned.

Talin spread the wound, but he could see nothing. Glancing around, he saw the courtyard was filling. Aliya and her ladies appeared at the main entrance to the palace. Dismissing her for the moment, he bellowed for a blade. A soldier rushed forward, thrusting a knife into his palm. Bracing himself, Talin grasped the blade and thrust it into Solly's belly, quickly slicing the flesh all the way around the wound and cutting the plug of flesh out. Solly cried out as the blade cut into him, passing beyond consciousness almost at once. When Talin had cut the piece from his flesh, he dropped the dagger, grabbed Solly's head and shook him. "I took it out," he growled. "You must make the wound close."

Rousing slightly, Solly frowned in concentration. Slowly, as Talin watched with a sense of profound relief, the blood ceased to pour from Solly's body and the wound began to close.

Shaken far more than he liked, Talin sat back on his heels, brushing the sweat that beaded his brow with the back of his hand.

"What has happened?" Aliya gasped.

Talin turned to her, his expression grim. "Your father does not want peace," he said tiredly. "He wants my blood."

Aliya stared at Talin in horror. "He did this? It can not be! He would not break the truce of a peace talk in this way!"

"There was no truce," Talin retorted grimly, pushing himself to his feet and bending to scoop up the lump of flesh he had cut from Solly. Lady Leesa's eyes rolled back in her head as he examined the bloody flesh and she wilted to the ground, taking Lady Beatrice, who tried to catch her, with her.

Talin glanced toward the pair curiously as he continued. "There would not have been if I had asked for it. Very likely they would have slain me on the spot if they had known who I was before I reached them."

Turning from her, he surveyed the men who'd come to gawk. "Reyhan--as soon as Solly is stronger, help him to his quarters."

Once Reyhan had acknowledged the order, he struck off across the practice yard purposefully.

Aliya glanced at her ladies, but absently. She followed Talin as he crossed the yard to retrieve the spear he'd dropped.

"How did you find him?" she asked anxiously.

"I followed the corpses."

Aliya blinked as if he'd slapped her. "He is a good man," she said shakily. "He would not do such things. He is just angry that you took me."

Talin stopped abruptly and turned to study her face intently. After a moment, he lifted a hand to caress her cheek. Discovering that it was bloodied, he dropped it to his side again. "I am sorry, Aliya," he said finally.

Turning, he left her, scanning the men who were loitering in the yard hoping to learn what had happened. "You," he bellowed finally to a group of three men who stood together. "Find the elders and send them to my council chambers."

Reaching the chamber, he moved to the wide window at one end and stood looking down at his mountain and the green valley at its feet where his people toiled in the fields. There would be no harvesting this year's crop if they were not quick about it. He had no trouble at all envisioning the lush fields churned and strewn with bodies as the fields of the wolf clan had been when he had seen them.

When the council had assembled, he turned away from the window at last, strode to the council table and dropped the spear and the flesh in the center of it. "We have our war," he announced grimly, "but I very much fear we are about to discover that we have only played into the hands of the man children."

The elders examined the objects he'd dropped on the table before them with varying expressions of surprise, disgust, and confusion. "What is this?" Malik, the high elder, demanded at last.

"Our extinction, unless I miss my guess," he retorted grimly.

Chapter Sixteen

"A spear?" Malik scoffed.

Talin leaned forward, bracing his palms on the table. "That is no ordinary spear, old man. I cut that from Solly after he took the spear meant for me," he added, nodding toward the piece of flesh that had already begun to rot--that seemed to decay before their eyes.

"Two days ago, I sent two of my best men--to their death, I fear. They were told to infiltrate the army the man children were forming, learn what they could of their plans and return with the information. They did not return. Last eve, Captain Solly and I went to discover why. When we reached the encampment, it was already deserted, for the army had moved into battle.

"The kingdom of Cavar is no more. It lies in ruin. The clan of the wolf is scattered, if any still live."

Stunned silence greeted his announcement. "That can not be!" Jenar, the youngest of the four elders, exclaimed.

"It *is*!" Talin bellowed, slamming his fist on the table for emphasis. "I saw it with my own eyes. King Matin's stronghold lay in ruin. His fields and forest were littered with the bodies of the man children, and his own people lay dead or dying among them. They did not rise again. They did not heal themselves. They could not."

Pushing away from the table, he moved to the window again, bracing his palms on the window ledge. "One I found who was still alive spoke of poison. When I pulled this spear from Solly, he swore it was still there and he could not close the wound."

"Magic," Malik said slowly. "They have found someone powerful if he can weave a spell of this magnitude." He frowned. "Why did they attack the clan of the wolf? I have heard of no animosity between Cavar and Anduloosa." He looked up at Talin as the king turned from the window to face him. "Only to test their magic?"

Talin's face hardened. "I do not think so. King Andor himself spoke of ridding these lands of the 'unnaturals.' We are not the only target of their fear and hatred. They mean to do all that is in their power to destroy all of the kingdoms of the man beasts."

"We must discover what we can of the potion used to wither the flesh of an immortal," Jenar said decisively. "We must find a wizard."

Talin's lips tightened. "We have never had need of such things," he pointed out. "You will not find one in this kingdom, nor likely any of the kingdoms of the man beasts."

"We must find one if we have to go into the lands of the man children."

"They *are* man children," Talin growled. "We could not pay enough to be assured of their loyalty. The man children have no honor when it comes to dealing with those they consider their enemies. Even supposing we could find one, he would take our coin and turn upon us the moment it suits his purpose to do so."

"Nevertheless," Malik put in abruptly, "we must prepare as we can. I have heard of a race in a distant land of learned, benign beings that are neither man child, nor man beast. They are seers, but though that is their greatest gift, they are also very intelligent and learned, as I have said. If anyone can help us to understand and perhaps fight the magic being used against us, then they will know, and they could be trusted. We will go and see what we can learn from them," he finished decisively.

"I have never heard of these beings," Jenar objected immediately. "Are we to simply wander about searching for a myth?"

"A distant land, you say?" Tiko demanded. "I am not at all certain that I could go so far. I do not have the strength I once had."

Grinding his teeth, Talin dismissed them and left them arguing the matter. He had met with his council, per law, and listened to their advice. Now he was free to do whatever he thought best without their interference. When he reached the practice yard once more, he climbed the stairs to the top of the wall and had the men summoned to assemble.

While he waited from them to form up and grow silent, he did a mental head count. The clan of the golden falcon was one of the largest of all the clans of man beasts, and yet their numbers were few when compared to any of the clans of the man children. He had two other strongholds that held perhaps as many together as had assembled here and he still feared it would not be enough, a thought so alien to him that it took him many moments even to arrive at why he found the count so disturbing.

It had never mattered before, he realized finally.

"We are at war with the tribes of the man children," he bellowed loudly enough that all could hear when they had finally quieted. The moment he made the announcement, however, they burst into ragged, gleeful cheers.

Grinding his teeth impatiently, he waited until some of the noise had died down again. "Make no mistake--this is no game we play at. This is not a fight to resolve some petty dispute, or a battle to relieve the boredom. We will be fighting for our right to exist."

A deathly silence fell as the men began to exchange baffled glances.

"The tribes of the man children spread upon this land like locusts, and they have united for the first time in known history with only one goal in mind--to destroy the clans of the man beast."

"We are far stronger!" someone bellowed from the crowd below. "It does not matter that they outnumber us."

"It *did* not matter," Talin corrected the man. "Solly was brought down by a single spear. They have gathered wizards to their cause who have concocted powerful potions against us. You must use the utmost caution when we go into battle and guard yourselves, else we will find death, not victory.

"I will need couriers--ten in all--to travel to the kings of the other clans and warn them before it is too late. The rest of you are to begin preparations for war."

"Are there not twelve clans?" someone called.

"Not any more," Talin retorted grimly. "The clan of the wolf is no more."

* * * *

Talin's thoughts were dark as he climbed the stairs to his own chambers. He had not liked to risk demoralizing his men with such an announcement, but it could not be helped. It would have been far worse to say nothing, for they were not accustomed to worrying overmuch about being wounded in battle. There was always the chance that a stray bolt or spear might pierce a throat or brain and cause too much damage to recover completely, or, in hand to hand combat, that they might have their head cloven from their body by a sword, but these were not things that happened often.

He knew his men. If he had said nothing, the youngest and wildest among them, particularly those who had not seen battle before, might have felt compelled to display their stupidity by seeing just how many wounds they could survive to brag about.

Despite his distraction, he had not failed to notice the subtle changes in the palace that indicated Aliya had indeed accepted her role.

Either that, or she had decided to annoy him by changing everything about, he thought wryly, for she had had the great hall completely rearranged--which he might not have noticed except for the fact that he'd run into furniture that had not been in his path before.

He still had not decided whether or not he should tell her her father had disowned her when he reached the door to his suite. Abruptly recalling the look of devastation on her face when she had asked about her father, he decided against it. He could think of no reason why she needed to know, and many why she shouldn't be told.

She was his concubine. He could simply refuse to allow her to see her father. She would be angry, but he thought that she would get over that. He wasn't so certain she would get over the discovery that the father she loved did not love her.

He was almost surprised to discover that the latch opened the door readily.

She was seated in the tub, bathing, and he stopped abruptly, feeling his throat close as he stared at the foaming water that revealed almost as much of her body as it concealed. With a strenuous effort, he dragged his gaze from her breasts to her face. Without even glancing at the maids attending her, he bellowed, "Out!"

Removing the tunic he wore, he strode toward the tub without waiting to see if they complied to the order or not, and discarded his loincloth, climbing into the tub with her.

She uttered a gasp, her eyes widening as he stepped into the tub with her.

The water crested the edge of the tub and washed over in a great wave as he settled, drawing shrieks of dismay from the maids that hadn't moved quickly enough. Ignoring them, and the slamming of the door behind them, Talin reached for Aliya and dragged her against him, covering her surprised mouth at the same moment.

As welcome heat surged through her blood, Aliya melted against Talin, entwining her arms around his neck to keep her water slick body from slipping away from his. The hungry possessiveness of his kiss wiped every thought from her mind. Only a dizzying need that quickly became a conflagration remained as her skin slipped along his in delightful friction and their bodies bumped together.

The heat of his mouth was nearly searing as he stroked his tongue possessively along hers and then coaxed her tongue into his own mouth, sucking it. Her body quaked at that, went up in flames.

She was shaking all over when he broke the kiss at last and moved his mouth along the tender skin of her throat and neck. His hands skated from her waist to her hips and down, cupping her buttocks and bringing her up onto his thighs. The tips of his fingers delved her cleft from behind as he lifted her against him. When she settled again, she felt his engorged member where his fingers had been moments before, gliding along her cleft with insistent pressure. Gasping, she tightened her arms around his neck, squeezing her eyes closed to hold the pleasure more tightly to her as he guided her in a slow rocking motion that touched off tremors of exquisite sensation.

Lifting her again after only a moment, he guided the head of his cock into the mouth of her sex, bearing down on her hips until her body began to slowly settle over his. She gasped, struggling to adjust to the intrusion.

He dragged her face down, kissed her lips briefly and then lifted her again, fastening his mouth over one nipple and sucking it until her belly began to clench and unclench around the flesh he'd embedded in her, kneading his cock rhythmically.

Uttering a groan, as if he was in pain, he released her nipple and surged upward, carrying her with him.

Aliya gasped, her eyes flying wide as his hands settled beneath her buttocks. Stepping from the tub, he moved to the bed, dropping her on the edge and thrusting again. A shiver went through her. She lifted her legs to wrap them around his waist and ground herself against him as she arched her head back. He caught her thighs, lifting her legs to his shoulders instead and thrusting again, deeper this time--deeper than she thought possible. His cock slid inside of her then, slamming almost painfully into her womb.

Cutting shards of pleasure sliced into her as he began pounding into her at a furious pace. The cool air barely tempered the feverish heat enveloping her skin in a rising conflagration. Her blood raced, her breath quickened. He thrust into her, groaning with pleasure which she echoed.

He ground against her clit, making her nerve endings riot with pleasurable waves of sensation. She moaned, clutching his back, digging her nails into his flesh and reveling in the feel of his powerful muscles flexing with each forceful thrust. He kissed her collarbone and neck, sucking at the delicate tendons lacing her neck, nipping at her collarbone, laving and kissing her everywhere he could reach. He crawled along her jaw with molten kisses until he reached her lips and covered them with his own. He forced her mouth wide, thrusting his tongue inside to tease and tangle with hers.

She sucked him hungrily, mindless with fervent need. His barely leashed savagery thrilled her, making her wetter with each gliding stroke until she began to sob with need.

His pace quickened, as if sensing her distress, raising her urgency tenfold. He tore his mouth away from her lips, grinding out her name in a rough voice.

Her body responded with equal fervor, racing upward, tightening, coiling for the leap she knew would come. And still she uttered a hoarse cry of keen gladness and surprise as her body began to convulse in hard waves of pleasure. He leaned over her, suckling first one nipple and then the other as the waves crested, broke and crested again.

She felt tight all over, every muscle shaking and trembling as the orgasm danced along her nerves, retreating and advancing until she thought she would explode.

When she went limp and breathless, he withdrew slightly and allowed her legs to slip to the floor. Before she had entirely grasped what he was about, he had rolled her onto her belly and entered her again. She gasped and arched her back, flinging her damp hair back. She gripped the sheets in fingers like claws as he began to thrust again, and her body, which had barely touched down, soared upward again in another race toward explosive release.

Even as she felt his body began to convulsive and his hot seed spilled into her channel, another harder climax caught her in its debilitating grip.

"Oh, Talin," she cried out, practically screaming his name as she collapsed beneath him.

She was barely conscious when Talin withdrew. As her legs trembled and threatened to give way, he scooped her up and climbed into the bed with her, sprawling half atop her.

She stroked his muscled, tense back soothingly as she caught her breath, enjoying the warm glow that enveloped her in the aftermath of their lovemaking, enjoying the feel of his body on hers. She tangled her fingers in his soft, golden hair, luxuriating in the closeness she felt with him. It dawned on her as she began to drift lazily, however, that there had been a reason why she had lain in wait for Talin, beyond the lovely outcome she had just enjoyed.

Weary from days of little or no sleep, and completely sated, for the moment at least, Talin was drifting blissfully toward sleep when Aliya pierced his bubble of contentment.

Chapter Seventeen

"Talin?"

"Hmmm?"

"Take me to my father," Aliya whispered coaxingly.

With an effort, Talin lifted one eyelid and stared at her warily. He had not expected it to come to this so soon, and he was not prepared for it. He sighed inwardly. "No."

She frowned. "I was not asking that you return me to my father," she said carefully. "My home is with you now. I accept that. It is only that ... I think if I can make him understand that I am well treated, that I am willing to stay, he will be willing to consider peace."

Talin stroked a hand down her soft, curling hair, smoothing it before twining a dark curl around one finger. "Do you?"

The question obviously distracted her, at least momentarily. She cocked her head questioningly.

"Accept?"

Her response was just hesitant enough to remind him of their last argument when she had shaken him by threatening to take a lover if he took a queen--as he would eventually have to, and he realized that he had not adequately considered the vast differences between them. Among his own kind, acceptance of a mate was irrevocable. Once a female had committed herself, she would not look at another and certainly would not allow another male to mate with her. As many times as he had seen the wanton behavior of the man children, he should have realized that they felt no such binding. He supposed he had. He had simply refused to believe that Aliya was the same.

"I have said that I do."

Talin's lips tightened. Without a great degree of success, he tried to tamp the anger that pricked at him. He removed his hand from her hair. "He would not believe that. He would think that I had threatened--or frightened--you into begging," he muttered irritably. "That would only lead him to the mistaken belief that I fear him, which I do not, and he would see it as a weakness he could exploit."

"He is not like that!" she exclaimed earnestly. "He is a man of reason. He will see that I am ... satisfied with you as my husband, and he will withdraw."

"Accept? Satisfied?" he growled, inexplicably hurt, and angry because he was. "Could you possibly be more tepid in your enthusiasm?"

Aliya stared at him blankly for several moments before her own anger erupted. "He would certainly know I was lying if I began to sing your praises!" she snapped. "He would more likely believe that my mind had snapped if I professed undying devotion for a man who had captured me and forced me to accept him!"

Talin bolted upright and got out of the bed. "I freely admit that I was wrong to steal you from your home, but you and I both know that I did not force myself upon you," he growled furiously. "You accepted me."

"I admitted that I did," she snapped petulantly, crossing her arms over her chest. "But you behave as if that is an insult."

He stared at her for a long moment, too stunned to speak. Finally, uttering a growl of frustration, he stalked away from the bed and snatched up the clothing he'd discarded. "We are not speaking of the same thing," he muttered.

"Well, I am certain I do not understand the fine difference!" she snapped, glaring at him when he glanced up from trying to figure out how to get his loincloth straightened.

"You accepted me as your mate. I distinctly heard you say 'I am yours' and now you speak as if you simply caved in to the inevitable because you could not avoid it. There is a very great difference between the two and I believe if you will give it a little thought you can figure that out."

It occurred to Talin as he slammed his chamber door behind him that he had managed to avoid the conversation he had feared Aliya would pry from him, the truth about her 'dear' father, but he found little comfort in the fact that he had spared her sensibilities while she had trampled all over his. Shrugging it off, he struggled into his tunic and stalked down stairs to join his men and watch their practice.

One had the audacity to look him over as he exited the palace and smirk.

Talin wiped it off the man's face with his fist.

He couldn't help but notice, though, that several men glanced at him curiously as he strode back and forth across the field and then looked away quickly again. Since, from what he could tell, they had all been outside and should not have been able to overhear any part of his most recent argument, he began to wonder what they found so fascinating about his attire.

It wasn't until he decided to abandon the practice field and go check on his captain that he realized his loincloth felt downright peculiar. Upon examining it, he discovered he had put it on backwards, which not only explained why his troops had found him so fascinating, but was proof positive that the woman was driving him out of his mind!

One look at Solly wiped every other thought from his mind. The man was still pale and so weak he could not even get out his bed. After glancing around the sparse room for something to sit on, Talin grabbed a stool and dragged it up to the bedside. "You are ill?"

"But I will live," Solly retorted, smiling faintly, "thanks to your quick thinking."

Talin shrugged it off. "And I live thanks to yours. If you had not caught the spear, I most certainly would have. Tell me how feel," he ended, changing the subject abruptly back to the wound.

Solly thought it over. "As weak as an infant, though not really ill."

Talin frowned. "You do feel as if there is poison in your body?"

"Nay. I am certain there is not."

Talin cupped his chin in one hand, thoughtfully stroking his lower lip with one finger. "The man beast spoke of poison."

Shrugging, Solly pushed himself upright, leaning back against the head board of his bunk. "Either he was wrong, or they have more than one trick for us."

Talin smiled wryly. "Thank you for pointing that out. I would have felt much better if I could believe that we had ferreted out the limits of their tricks. But I fear you are right. They will have other unpleasant surprises for us, perhaps something different for each of the clans to exploit their particular weakness?"

"We have a weakness?" Solly asked, genuinely surprised.

Shaking his head, Talin grimaced. "Beyond arrogance? We are not immortal in the sense that we can not be killed at all. It is only that we are far harder to kill than the man children and thus longer lived. You may be certain that they know all of our weaknesses, perhaps even better than we do. This is not something that abruptly erupted. They have been planning this for a very long time, storing their hatred of us, preparing for it and they have caught us completely off guard."

Solly frowned. "What of the other clans?"

"I sent couriers to warn them, but it is anyone's guess if they will pay it any heed. We are none of us on the best of terms. And that is another weakness the man children will be certain to exploit, for they have joined forces against us."

"To a man, we are still worth ten of them," Solly pointed out.

"They have twenty … or more. And they have sorcery, as well. The tainted flesh I cut from your body withered before my eyes. There was nothing natural in that. It was magic, the blackest, and if I had not thought to do what I did, very likely your body would have withered just as quickly. We are not facing the possibility of losing one man, or a handful, to the horde. We must plan our strategy carefully else we will be overrun as surely as the clan of the wolf was."

Solly frowned. "Armor, you think?"

Talin considered it, as he had before, but again dismissed it. "It would weigh us down too much, dangerously so. We would lose speed and agility even if we only used enough to shield the most vulnerable areas of our bodies. Moreover, we can not be certain the sacrifice of maneuverability would even be worth it. The armor the man children wear will not stop a well place arrow or spear."

Solly nodded thoughtfully, as if he, too, had considered that aspect but had not thought of anything else to suggest. "We are safe here, I believe," he said musingly.

Talin sent him a questioning look.

"The royal palace is the least accessible of all of your holdings. We should gather our people here to protect the young and the weak."

Talin stood abruptly and began to pace the room. "I would agree if not for the threat of wizards. We do not know how powerful they might be. I would not like to think that I had gathered everyone together to make it easier for my enemy to destroy my clan." He waved a hand dismissively.

"For now, we will leave that. Our mountains have always protected us. We will look for them to do so now. I had planned to meet King Andor's army on the plain below and fight them in hand to hand combat. Now I see that that would have been foolhardy. We would have been overrun by the combined armies of the man children in no time at all, for we would not even have the advantage of our strength in healing with the magic they use.

"I will set the men to building retaining walls along the mountainside and filling them with rocks to be released to protect the palace if we can not turn them away before that. I believe they will come directly here, but there is no guarantee they will not try to take the smaller fortresses first. They will have to prepare also.

"We must make certain that we have plenty of stone for an aerial bombardment, which I hope will drive them away before they is any real threat, but I will feel better, I think if we find a place of safety for those of our clan most vulnerable and least able to defend themselves--the very young, the very old, and females who are with child."

"What am I to do, Sire?" Solly asked.

Talin studied him for a long moment. "Rest, for now. I will have need of you. When you feel strong enough, you will oversee the fortifications. I will go myself and check the defenses of the other strongholds and then I will find a place of safety for our people."

* * * *

As stunned as she was by Talin's outburst, she was more thoughtful than angry after he had gone. She had insulted him. She had no doubt of that. She just wasn't certain how she had insulted him. She did give his parting shot a good bit of thought, but turn it though she might, she didn't see the difference.

She began to think there was no difference, that he had deliberately started the argument only to distract her from something else, for, after she thought it over she distinctly recalled that there had been wariness in his eyes when she had first broached the subject of speaking directly with her father. The question was, why did he not want her to speak with her father?

He had suggested that it would reflect badly on his manhood and his honor, but she didn't believe that he was worried for a moment that anyone would think he was a coward. No one who knew him could think that. She had not known him a full month and she knew he was never hesitant to put himself at the forefront.

He had almost gotten himself killed going into an enemy encampment unarmed and with only Solly at his side. Foolhardy, he might be, but he was certainly not lacking in bravery or spirit!

Undoubtedly, he had only said that to distract her.

She supposed he didn't trust her. She could not find that she really blamed him. She thought he should have realized by now that she had more honor than to betray him in such a way, but trust was something one felt, an emotion. Like faith, love, and even hate, it did not necessarily follow rules of logic.

It irritated her, though, that he refused even to allow her to speak to her father. Her father certainly had no reason to trust him, or to believe any message she might send by him. If she could see him face to face, speak with him, and he could see that she was content with the way things had turned out, then he would be reasonable. He had only wanted to see her settled with a man that she could admire and respect, a man who was strong and brave and capable. She knew her father despised the man beasts in a general way, but she felt that he was not unreasonable in his dislike. If he would only take the time to get to know Talin, he would see that Talin had far more virtues than faults.

He had taken her captive and she had been both furious and frightened by that, but she had come to realize that most of that was because she had expected him to behave as most men did--without any consideration for her. Not only had he not assaulted her as she had expected, he had gone out of his way to see to her comfort and well being, nearly getting himself killed in the raid to bring her her most valued possessions.

Talin was right. She had not simply given in to the inevitable. She had welcomed him and felt right in the giving of herself to him.

He wasn't angry, she realized abruptly. He was hurt. He had taken the time to coax her to come to him willingly and she had refused to admit it--because it made her feel better about herself if she refused to acknowledge how quickly she had fallen under his spell.

Did yielding to him so quickly make her less than she should have been though? A woman of weak morals and mind? Or was it a case of instinctively recognizing that Talin had all of the qualities any woman could wish for in a husband and accepting that she was not likely to find a better mate?

She *had* been primed to search for a mate when he had come into her life. In truth, she had been over primed. She had been waiting anxiously for her father to settle her since her sixteenth birthday. If she had been anyone else, even the daughter of an aristocrat, she would probably have been settled already.

She frowned at that thought, wondering if she had simply been 'ripe for the plucking' and that had made her easy prey. After a little thought, though, she dismissed that. She had been courted most assiduously, and she had not felt at any time that she was in danger of losing control of her desires. She could not think of one man, in point of fact, that had stirred even her interest in that way.

Would it be best, she wondered, to try to soothe the injury she had inadvertently inflicted when Talin returned? Or better to go and find him and try to explain?

She was not going to ask her ladies for any more advice, she decided, eyeing them with disfavor when they returned at last to clean up the mess she and Talin had made in his suite.

"It did not work," she said to Lady Beatrice, climbing from the bed and moving to the tub to bathe off quickly before she dressed.

Lady Beatrice's brows rose. "I thought not. I heard him bellowing, though I must say the walls are very thick here. I did not catch the meat of the conversation."

"Perhaps you should try putting your ear to the door next time?" Aliya snapped irritably.

Lady Beatrice reddened. "I had not thought of that, your grace."

Aliya sent her a disbelieving glance, but decided not to pursue it. "I think he is concerned that I would betray his trust and stay with my father if he allowed me to go to speak with him. He refused to consider it."

Beatrice and Leesa exchanged a look. Aliya caught it, but she couldn't entirely interpret it. "If your father offered you sanctuary, you would consider it, though?"

Aliya frowned. "What do you mean 'if'?"

The maids exchanged another look. "She did not mean if he did," Leesa said firmly. "She was only asking if you would consider it ... if you had the chance."

Aliya stared at Leesa for several moments before she turned to study Beatrice. "You mean lie to Talin? Give him my word that I would only be going to try to negotiate peace and then betray him and stay with my father?"

"You are a captive! You owe him no loyalty!"

"I am his concubine!"

Beatrice gaped at her.

"A devil's concubine!" Lady Leesa spat in disgust. "He has dishonored you!"

"Do not *dare* to speak of him that way!" Aliya said furiously. "In the eyes of King Talin, and his people, he has placed me in a respectable position as his wife--not his queen and I can not say that I am happy with all of their customs--but he treats me with respect and so do his people. It is not a disgrace and I will not behave as if I feel any shame!"

"He tricked you! You told us that!" Lady Leesa exclaimed.

Aliya stared at her with a mixture of embarrassment and anger. "Do not be a fool or behave as if I am one! The truth is that, whether he did it on purpose or not, he was kind enough to give me an excuse to do what I wanted to do and still save face! If I had not wanted to, no trick he could have devised would have ensnared me. If it had not mattered to me whether he lived or died, I would not have wanted to offer him the comfort he asked for!

"He deceived me, yes, and I am still angry because I felt so foolish when I realized my mistake, but I can not lay all the blame for that at his door. I was not thinking clearly because I was so upset. I know who and what he is--a man beast--and yet I behaved as if he were just the same as we are--because to me he is.

"Poor man. It is sad, really, that he was willing to endure so much only to have me fuss over him." She thought back over it for several moments and bit her lip, and then a snort of amusement escaped her and she burst out laughing. "You should have seen his face when I asked him if he wanted more gruel," she gasped weakly after several moments, mopping the tears from her eyes.

Lady Beatrice stared at her as if she had grown two heads. "King Andor was right. The fear has turned your mind!"

Aliya's amusement vanished abruptly. "Posh! I am not afraid of Talin. I do not think I ever was. If I had not been so terrified of flying through the air I think I would have been far more thrilled than frightened when he captured me so daringly and snatched me right from under father's nose. It was ... romantic."

"Romantic!" Lady Leesa gasped. "You have been listening to far too many bard's tales! Was it not romantic enough to suit you to have the rulers of so many kingdoms vying for your hand in combat?"

Aliya gave her a look. "That was politics and I do not find politics particularly romantic since it is all about lands and money and allies when there is war. To be sure, if it had not been Talin and instead was someone not nearly as handsome, brave, and sweet, I probably would not have thought it was romantic to be a captive bride, but it *was* Talin. And although I have given it a great deal of thought, I am not convinced I would have been as content with the man who won me by 'right of might.' At least four were either far too old to compete themselves, or infirm, and what if their champion had won the day?"

She shook her head at her ladies. "I was born to my station, but I am still a woman. I would have done my duty, but I would not have been content. I know father wanted to settle me well, and he is unhappy now, and angry. But I think if he saw that I am happy and well treated and respected he would not make war. That is all I wanted to do--speak to him and try to settle the dispute between Talin and my father peacefully.

"I could not leave Talin now if I wanted to. And I do not want to."

Her ladies exchanged a glance. "You could not make peace by telling your father that. You have no idea how grieved and enraged he was when he discovered that you had been taken by one of the very devils he despises so much. The only thing that *might* appease your father is if you returned to him, begged for his forgiveness, and agreed to wed whomever he could negotiate a marriage with."

Chapter Eighteen

Aliya merely stared at her two ladies, whom she had long thought of as friends, numb with shock as what they told her sank slowly into her mind and feeling as if she had never truly known any of the people she had cared for.

"It seems unfair, I know, when it was not your fault, but such is the way of the world. A woman must always take the blame. It is the woman who is defiled and then despised for it. And the unnaturals are so hated, it would almost have been better if he had been one of our own kind," Lady Beatrice spoke earnestly. "There are those who would still be willing to wed you still--after a suitable time, of course, once it is seen that you do not carry the seed of these abominations."

Aliya found she could not even catch her breath. Hurt and anger mingled so liberally inside of her she wasn't certain which was uppermost, but she felt as if she had been battered physically, not just verbally. "You are saying my father...?" she asked faintly.

Lady Leesa took her cold hand. "He mourns you as one lost to him."

"He would rather I was dead?" Aliya asked in disbelief.

"You *are* dead to him if you choose his enemies, for he has made an oath that he will not rest until he has cleansed the land of these creatures … and their kin."

Aliya retreated into her own thoughts, hardly aware of her ladies as they helped her dress and then settled her on a bench and combed and arranged her hair. When they had finished, she dismissed them.

Once they had gone, she moved to the window that looked down upon the courtyard and stood peering down at the practice field, wondering if Talin was among his men. She did not see him.

The maids who had served her until Talin had raided her father's palace to bring her own maids to her, came into the room to clean up. Moving away from the window, she settled in the chair near the hearth and watched them absently while their worked. "Is the king in the great hall?" she asked finally.

Both maids stopped and looked at her and then abruptly bobbed a curtsey. "He has left the castle, your grace," the younger of the two volunteered.

Aliya managed a faint smile of apology. "I am sorry that I did not ask before--by what name are you known?"

The girl smiled back at her shyly, but somewhat nervously. "I am called Lilith."

"How pretty! And you?"

The older girl blushed. "Maida."

"You are certain that he left the palace, Lilith?"

"Aye, your grace. Talk is we are at war and he has gone to oversee the fortifications of his other holdings."

Disappointment filled Aliya. "Then he is not likely to return for many days," she said, more to herself than the maids, who merely shrugged uncomfortably.

It would almost have been better, she thought, if there had not been a very good reason why he had left, matters of state that required his attention, for then she would have had a better idea of whether she, or rather their argument, had had anything to do with his decision. As it was, she couldn't begin to guess. To her, it seemed Talin was not the sort ever to delegate those things he considered of utmost importance. He preferred to ensure that all was done exactly as he wanted it done by overseeing it personally and not relying on reports and couriers and the like.

It was not the way her father did things, and she had thought it peculiar at first, but it seemed to her that Talin had no difficulty maintaining his authority despite that penchant. Moreover, it was patently clear that he was very dear to his people, that they felt a bond with him, even as their ruler, that her father did not with his own people.

How well, she wondered, had she really known her father?

It was true that he was tied up with affairs of state more often than not and spent little time with her beyond those occasions when they were together in formal settings, but she could not recall that he had ever lost his temper with her. He had always seemed so kind, so patient, even when she was a young child. He had not showered her with a great deal of affection. Physical displays of affection were so rare than she was almost as stunned as she was thrilled when he kissed her cheek or forehead, or patted her hand, but he had always been generous with his gifts. She could not even think of anything that she had wanted at any time that had not been promptly given.

Where had the cold, unfeeling, merciless man that her ladies described been hiding all this time?

Her mind simply could not seem to grasp that he had disowned her, and only because she had been taken captive by a man he considered his enemy and 'soiled' by that man's touch? She was condemned and despised on assumptions?

It happened to be true, now, but she had a feeling that it would have been the same if she had been returned to him a maiden still.

The love she had always believed was hers, unconditionally, had vanished in a puff of smoke. She felt more lost and confused than hurt. She supposed the real pain would come later, once the shock had worn off, but she was having trouble even dealing with the shock.

Shaking off her thoughts as the maids finished and turned to go, she addressed them again. "Do you know who did the shutters?"

Lilith nodded. "The master carpenter, Silo by name."

"Would you ask him to come to speak with me about the shutters?"

"Right away, your grace," the girl said, bobbing a curtsey and scurrying from the room.

When the maids had left, she rose and moved to the door, moving along the hall until she reached the next room, where her ladies had been settled. Pushing the door open, she went in and examined it. It was about half the size of the room she had been sharing with Talin, but when she moved to the windows, she discovered that the only two the room boasted looked out over the courtyard. "I expect this room was intended to be the queen's room, but I believe I would like to use it as a solar," she announced to no one in particular. "The view is … more to my liking and the windows are facing south so they will catch light most of the day."

She turned and studied Lady Leesa and Lady Beatrice for a moment. "You should gather your belongings and go to the housekeeper for other accommodations."

A man who appeared around middle age appeared at the door, drawn to the room, she supposed, by the sound of voices. She saw that he was carrying a tablet of some sort, or a book with loose pages carefully tucked between the hard backing. "You sent for me, your grace?" he asked, bowing when she turned to acknowledge his presence.

Aliya beamed at him. "You are Silo? The master carpenter?"

He bowed again. "At your service, your grace."

"I would like these shutters removed," she said, gesturing toward the windows. "They have a very pleasant view and it is far too gloomy in the palace with all of the windows covered. I have decided to make this my solar, and will need the beds removed and replaced with some comfortable benches. Perhaps a day bed, as well--oh, and a comfortable chair for Talin in case he decides to join me here sometime."

She glanced at her ladies. "When you speak to the housekeeper, have her send along the maids best at stitching. I will require pillows and cushions to add comfort."

"And stools," she added to Silo as she turned and headed out of the door.

He followed her, looking a little bewildered.

Pausing on the threshold, Aliya surveyed the room critically. "It is so gloomy in here. It must distress Talin! He was accustomed to the room being light and airy." She glanced at Silo apologetically. "He knows I find the prospect from the windows very unnerving, for I am accustomed to plains, not mountains. But there are two windows that look out over the practice field and the wall. Those need not be shuttered at all, and I am thinking that, perhaps, you could shutter only the lower half of the other windows, for I am very short and would not have to face the intimidating view myself. And it would allow a good deal more light into the room."

Silo surveyed her as if judging her height and moved to the windows she'd indicated. After studying them for several moments, he nodded. "We will have to take them down to cut them and move the hinges lower. Perhaps it would be best to begin with the solar? Then we can complete the work there and you would be comfortable while we worked in here."

"A very good suggestion," Aliya agreed, smiling. "Do you think that you could have all of this done by the time the king returns?" she asked, wondering if the man might have some idea of how long Talin would be gone.

Silo frowned thoughtfully. "It would not take long to take down the shutters and remove the furnishings that are there--a few hours only. I have several new benches that I can show you. If you like them they would be a start on refurnishing the room. If it meets your approval, then we could start in here the following morning. The king has gone to check the defenses on his other holdings and most likely will not be back for at least two or three days."

As disappointing as it was that he would be gone so long, it wasn't nearly as bad as she had thought. "Wonderful! He will be pleased, don't you think?" she asked hopefully.

Silo grinned. "I am sure of it, your grace."

He had already begun to turn away to rush off when he frowned and turned back. "I had not had the chance to speak with the king about these plans I have been working on, but he said that it was for you and it seems it would be best to consult you about them anyway."

Aliya stared at him in surprise when he opened the book he was carrying, glanced around and then moved to a table to spread out the drawings inside. Embarrassment flooded her when she saw her crude drawing on top of the stack, especially when she saw his neat, carefully drawn sketches beneath. "This has presented a challenge, your grace, a real challenge. The king brought this to me and said he knew that you missed your garden and he wanted to please you by building one here, but we are very high--very high and this is not good for plants because the nights are very cool, the winters long and spring very short. Added to that, you are naturally uncomfortable about being so high. But I believe I have come up with something that will work very well all the way around.

"It would be very small," he added uncomfortably, "at least at first, but if it does as well as I hope and you are happy with it, we can always enlarge it later and there would be room even in the small area to erect a small sitting area with an arbor as you have drawn here," he ended, tapping at the picture.

From out of no where tears arose, flooding Aliya's eyes and making the drawing waver. "He asked you to build a garden for me?" she asked disbelievingly. "When?"

Silo stared at her in dismay for several moments and scratched his chin uneasily. "Not long after you came. He was very anxious to make you feel comfortable. He said that he knew it was very different for you here and that you missed the things familiar. Uh--you are not pleased with the drawings?"

Aliya sniffed, brushed away the tears that were blinding her and nodded. "Yes. That is, I am not sure what this is, but I would love to have a garden."

When he had explained that he would erect high walls and then form a frame above them that would be a roof made up of windows to allow light and air in, Aliya was impressed. "This is a wonderful notion! They will have light and air and rain to nurture them and the braziers here and here should keep the plants warm. I am sure this will work!"

She frowned after a moment. "I will look forward to this, but I am not at all certain that this is something you should be devoting time to just now. Soon there will be war," she finished uncomfortably wondering what the castle folk thought of her when they must know she was the reason they were going to war.

Silo nodded. "I will speak with the king when he returns and tell him you have approved the drawings and we can begin whenever he likes."

When Silo had gone, she wandered around the room listlessly for a time and finally stopped to peer at the sliver of view she had of the practice field, fighting the urge to weep and wondering why in the world she even felt like weeping.

Talin's thoughtfulness pleased her. She couldn't imagine why it also made her want to cry.

After dwelling rather fondly over his thoughtfulness for some time, though, it dawned on her that Talin had spoke with her father and yet he had said nothing about the animosity her father felt toward her now. Had her father said nothing to him about it, she wondered?

He would not have refrained, she realized after a little thought. When faced with the man he despised for taking his daughter, she knew her father would not have even tried to refrain from venting his spleen.

That was why Talin had looked at her with such pity when she had been trying to defend her father's actions. That was why he had refused to allow her to speak to her father, refused even to explain why he wouldn't allow it.

He had been trying to protect her from the hurt he had known she would feel if she learned her father had denounced her!

She burst into tears then, allowing herself the luxury of mourning the loss of her home and father as she had not since she had been taken captive. They were well and truly lost to her now. She had not really accepted that before. Even when she had realized that her father would not be able to rescue her, in the back of her mind she had not really believed she would never see him or her home ever again.

Now she knew she wouldn't. He hated her only because he thought she had lain with Talin. Once he discovered that she had accepted Talin, welcomed him, he would never forgive her.

After a time, she dried her tears and washed her face. It would be hard, but she would learn to live with it. It would be harder still to live with the war on her conscience. She must try to reason with Talin when he returned, she decided. If her father had disowned her, she couldn't change that, but if he had, then he had no reason that she could see to make war either.

* * * *

Talin did not linger at Janpur, the smallest of his holdings. The keep was in good repair and already as ready as it could be to withstand an attack--which was to say hardly prepared. It was manned by only a handful and although built of stone, it had no inner ward, no battlement walls. It would not withstand much of an assault and could not be prepared for one in the little time available to them. Leaving orders that they were not to perform in any manner save as an outpost to alert him if the army moved upon this side of his holdings, Talin left to examine Kainrn, which guarded his northern boundary.

Built originally as the primary residence of his father, it was almost as large, and nearly as well fortified as the royal palace he had built for himself at his southern boundary, Tetan. Here he lingered for several days, spending the first examining the structure itself, the second overseeing the laying in of weapons and supplies, and the third running his men through their paces to see how well they performed in the armor he had sent men out to collect from the battlefields.

The results were disheartening. They were not accustomed to fighting in armor, even in their human form, and they were slow and clumsy. Deciding that, perhaps, it was only a matter of adjusting the armor to better fit them and practice, he ordered them to continue practicing until they could fight as well with the armor as without. Since he considered the possibility was not particularly remote that they would find themselves fighting hand to hand whether they liked it or not, he sent scouts to study the battle tactics of the man children.

One of the couriers he had sent out to warn the other clans arrived at Kainrn as he was preparing to return to Tetan with the news that Maxim, the King of the clan of the bears, had requested a meeting at the temple of the old gods in the land of Memnon. Talin frowned. "King Blain is agreeable to this?"

The courier nodded. "It was he who summoned everyone"

Talin lifted his head and stared into the distance. "The Wyvern?" he asked.

"The Wyvern themselves are under attack now. The man children marched through the lands of the dragon clan two days ago."

Talin looked at the man sharply. "You are certain?"

The courier's expression grew more grim. "As certain as I can be, sire. The land is in ruins. The old king's palace is burning."

Talin uttered a curse. "They are mad! Why destroy Memnon when the Wyvern had already wiped out most of the dragon clan in the war they have waged these many years? And how could they have reached Memnon anyway? The army was many days west and south of there when I last saw them. They could not move so great an army so fast on foot."

"This army came from across the sea and marches to join the other."

Talin gazed toward Tetan although he could not see the towers in the distance. "When is this meeting to take place?"

Chapter Nineteen

Near the place where once had stood an altar to the old gods, in the ruin of the great temple near the summit of Mount Carceras, a great fire blazed. Torches had been lit, as well, and created a wide ring of light around the central blaze. As Talin circled, drifting lower and lower, he saw that Maxim had not come alone to the meeting place.

He was the last to arrive.

Mentally, he shrugged. He had had things of great importance to attend to first and, in any case, he had not felt his presence was necessary while the others argued and slowly came to the same conclusion that he had--the time had come to set their differences aside and unite against a common foe.

The fact that they were still here seemed to indicate that they had finally agreed on that much anyway.

Alighting, he shifted, making his way toward the circle of stones and passing beneath the stone arch that had once formed the entrance to the old temple.

Most of the faces he recognized--the rulers of the clans of the Great Bear, the Panther, the Lynx, the Leopard, the Fox, and the Wyvern, and his closest brothers, and enemies, clans of the Eagle and the Condor. Some, he did not, but he sensed the presence of their beasts.

The high king, Balian, the last of his kind, stood apart from all the others.

Never in memory had all of the clans of man beasts come together in one place before now.

"You are late," Balian growled, his voice low, gravelly.

Talin sent him a speculative glance. "And yet, you are all here."

"We have been waiting many hours, and none of us particularly easy in our minds about this meeting," Blasien, king of the Leopard clan said irritably. "The man children would rejoice to find us all here together."

"They are still far from this place. I thought it wise to reconnoiter before I came."

"And you think we did not?" Raphael, of the clan of the wolf snarled.

Talin shrugged. "Like you, I prefer to know myself rather than only to accept what I am told. I had not thought that I would see you here."

Raphael scowled. "I make no apology for surviving, if that is what you are getting at."

"Do not take me up. I did not say that to start a quarrel between us." Talin glanced around the circle. "As it happens, I am glad to see your ugly face among those gathered here. I assume that is why we have all come? Because we all know that our chances of survival depend upon our unity?"

"Assumptions can easily lead to misconceptions," the king of the Wyvern purred. "I am only come because I am curious to see what has you all quaking."

Talin sent Vattin a cold stare. He respected Balian as the most powerful among them, the high king, but he had not been particularly fond of the folk of the dragon clan. Regardless, he felt sickened to find himself in the company of one so cold blooded as to hound an entire clan to the grave. To make war was one thing, but no dispute was excuse enough to warrant that much vindictiveness.

For that matter, he wasn't completely comfortable with most of those he meant to ally himself with--but he would, for his people. "By all means, meet the man children alone on the battle field. No one here will try to persuade you otherwise," he retorted coldly. "You have a wizard, have you not? With him, and your brave troops, perhaps you can chase off the man children for the rest of us and we can all go home?"

Vattin reddened as the mark struck home, for he was well aware that he was almost universally despised for having brought in a wizard to stack the odds in his favor in his war against the dragon clan. "Mortiver is dying."

Talin's brows rose. "So it is a little more than curiosity that brings you."

Vattin surged to his feet with a growl of rage.

"Settle!" Balian roared. "If we begin to fight among ourselves we are doomed."

Talin and Vattin glared at each other for many moments. Finally, Vattin settled again. When he did, Talin turned his back on him and moved to an opening in the circle.

"I believe their intent is to converge upon the great plain," he said, glancing around at the others. "Once the two armies join, I believe our chances of beating them will be diminished."

"How many days?" Raphael demanded.

Talin shrugged. "You could answer that better than I. My army moves through sky." After looking around, he pulled a branch from the fire and used the charred tip to draw a crude map upon the stones beneath their feet. "King Andor is here. My guess is that he has caught the blood lust and deviated from the original plan, for he has moved his army more west than north and east. The other army landed here on the coast and is traveling almost due west.

"There is only one kingdom of man beast near King Andor's position at this time, though, and his army is poised near their border. Unless the clan of the Fox manage to put up more of a fight than those who have already fallen, the army will be on the march again in two days time. So … two days, plus however many days it would take to move an army of that size overland."

One of those present that Talin hadn't recognized, spoke. "I am Sylvan, of the clan of the Fox," he introduced himself. "The man children will meet no resistance in the land of Modictia for, upon the advice of Raphael and Maxim, I have removed my army and my people from their path. A handful, only, remain to give the appearance that there is prey for them there. I do not think we can count upon them remaining there for more than a day."

Raphael, Maxim of the Great Bear clan, and Blasien moved closer, studying the map intently.

"If they continue on that path, they will crush Croaten between them in a week at the most," Blasien said. He glanced at one of the men gathered that was unknown to Talin. "Hadrian, these are your lands, what think you?"

"The terrain will slow foot soldiers and wagons, I am sure. And much of it is wasteland--they will find little food or water. I am condor, however, and know no more about the time it would take to move an army across than King Talin."

"Andor is not heading west," Vattin put in, giving Talin a hard look. "He is heading directly toward Goldone. Is that not so, Talin?"

Talin glared at the man. "It is not," he said coldly. "If it were, I would certainly have said so as it would not be in the best interests of my clan to do otherwise."

The men around the fire all exchanged glances, but it was Raphael who spoke. "You must learn not to judge others by yourself," he growled. "It leads one to misconceptions."

"What the hell do you mean by that?" Vattin snarled.

"The woman means nothing to them," Balian said coldly. "If all of this was only about the Princess Aliya, there would have been no need to gather all of their armies together and there certainly would not have been any reason to attack the clan of the wolf, or the Wyvern. The people of the man beast clans need your army, Vattin. They are seasoned from countless years of war, more so than many others who have done little more than skirmishing for years. Set aside your differences. There will be time, later, for us to fight among ourselves--*if* we fight together now. If not...." He shrugged. "Talin is right. We may all join my ancestors and live on only in memory."

* * * *

Aliya had run the gamut of emotions several times before she at last heard the sounds she had been waiting for that told of Talin's return. She had not been idle. Partly this was because she had been far too restless to remain so without feeling as if hysteria was closing in upon her. Most of it, though, was because she had convinced herself that the best way to assure Talin that she had accepted her role in his life was to show him she thought of the palace at Tetan as her home.

When she had done what she could with the royal suite, which no longer included a bed chamber for the master and a separate one for the mistress, but rather a single sleeping chamber for them both and a solar that they could use as a private retreat, she tracked down the chamberlain. They needed rich fabrics to soften the harshness of stone walls, floors, and ceilings. Almost reluctantly, he had led her to the king's storerooms.

The cavernous room, she discovered, was filled almost from floor to ceiling with more riches than she had seen in her lifetime--all collecting dust.

Ignoring the man's protests that most of it had been stored since Talin's mother's time and that the king had no interest in such frivolities, she had promptly begun emptying the room of paintings, wall hangings, and carpets; goblets, plate, pitchers, and platters of silver and gold, encrusted with bright gems; and ornately carved and crafted, tables, chairs, chests and armoires, working the palace servants from daylight till dusk.

In the back of her mind, she spent much of that time castigating herself for focusing on something so inconsequential and unnecessary as beautifying the palace when they were on the brink of war. She realized after a little time, though, that it had as bracing an effect on the nerves of the castle folk as it did hers. They found comfort in the very fact that it was so completely frivolous. They had less time to think and worry about the threat looming over them, and the brightening and beautification of their immediate surroundings lightened their spirits.

Unable to remain suitably dignified and wait in her suite for Talin to come to her, and fearful, truth be told, that he might not linger but instead leave again almost at once, Aliya hurried down the tower stairs to the great room as soon as she was certain that it was Talin who had arrived and not someone else. She arrived at one entrance to the great hall, breathless, at almost the same moment that Talin entered the great hall from the courtyard entrance.

Plainly distracted, he was half way across the great hall when he came to an abrupt halt as if he had only then noticed that something was different. A twinge of uneasiness went through Aliya as he began to look around the great hall as if he had never seen it before and wondered if he had wandered into the wrong place. It occurred to her forcefully for the first time that she had not even asked his permission to make the changes she had, or asked if Talin would mind her removing his treasures from storage. She had, in fact, ignored the chamberlain when he had suggested that Talin might not like it and behaved as if she had every right to do whatever she pleased.

When Talin at last met her gaze across the distance that still separated them, she felt guilt creep into her face, though she tried her best to appear unconcerned.

She could tell nothing about his expression, but after a moment, he headed directly toward her.

She was still trying to decide whether to race back up the stairs and bar the door to the solar or stand her ground when Talin stopped in front of her. "I have missed you," she said a little weakly.

Some of the tension seemed to leave him. A faint smile curled his lips. "I can not imagine where you found the time."

That was not precisely the reaction she had been hoping for, but at least he did not seem angry. "Even so."

Slipping his arms around her, he pulled her close. "I have missed you more," he murmured, nudging her chin up with his hand and covering her lips hungrily.

As acutely self-conscious as she was of the audience they had in the great hall, Aliya discovered her shyness did not outlast the heat of that kiss. Warmth flowed through her veins like honeyed wine, stirring her senses to a sharpness that detected the faintest of touches with every labored breath they took. When he broke the kiss and swept her into his arms in a dizzying swirl of motion and started up the stairs, she could only cling to him, resting her head against his shoulder.

Instead of setting her on her feet when they reached the suite, Talin kicked the door closed behind then and strode to the bed, climbing onto the mattress with her still clutched against his chest and settling heavily against her even as he laid her on the mattress. Covering her mouth at once, he kissed her as he traced the fitted bodice of her gown. Reaching down, he grabbed a handful of fabric and tucked her skirt around her waist, exposing her legs and belly. Cool air caressed her through the thin fabric of her undergarments and then brushed her bare skin as he thrust the confining fabric out of his way.

Anxious to feel the touch of his hands on her bare skin, Aliya reached behind her back and tugged at the ribbon that secured her bodice, loosening it only fractionally. It still restricted her ribs, making it difficult to breathe as her heart began racing with excitement.

Abandoning his exploration of her belly, Talin slipped his hand upward again, scooping one breast from her bodice. As he dragged his mouth from hers and covered the puckered tip of the beast, he reached down again, searching for the opening he had unearthed before in her under garments.

Aliya gasped as he found it, his clever fingers sending sharp stabs of pleasure through her as he parted the tender flesh of her woman's mound and teased the tiny, exquisitely sensitive bud of flesh there. Desire seemed to pour through her in a fiery tide from both points, colliding in her belly. Moisture gathered inside of her clenched sex. Her body began to quake and shudder with the need to feel him filling her.

"Talin!" she gasped, arching against his hand, digging her hands into the mattress.

Lifting his head from her breast, he surged over her, parting her thighs with his knee and settling his hips between hers. She arched against him, silently pleading with him to ease her distress.

She nipped at his shoulder and then sucked it as she felt the head of his cock slipping into her wetness, stretching her. Her hips seemed to come up off the bed of their own accord, pressing forward to sheath his hard flesh.

The building pressure eased as he ceased to push, withdrew slightly. She dug her head into the mattress, arching her neck, lifting her hips to receive him when he thrust again. Blindly, she clawed at the mattress as he moved deeper inside of her, panting for breath as her body adjusted to his possession, clutched at him.

Burrowing his face against her neck, he slipped an arm around her tightly and thrust again, began a rhythm of thrust and retreat that was the sweetest of sword plays. Gasping, groaning, she joined him in battle, parrying each thrust with her hips, demanding more with the movements of her body.

Gasping hoarsely, he gave, began to race toward the summit they both struggled toward at a desperate pace. A keen cry was wrenched from her throat as her body reached its peak and broke apart in crashing waves of rapture, convulsing so hard it sent him over the edge to join her in the expenditure of bliss.

The explosion and the shock waves in its aftermath seemed to drain her of every ounce of energy. Limp, totally sated, Aliya struggled to catch her breath as Talin relaxed heavily against her.

Slowly, her heart ceased to hammer so frantically it felt as if it would explode. Her lungs stopped to labor for breath.

Drowsy in the aftermath of their lovemaking, she tried to block everything from her mind and reach for the comfort of sleep. When Talin moved away from her at last and then slipped from the bed and began to dress, however, sleep evaded her. She lay still for a few moments, but she found she could not bear for him to leave without speaking with him.

"You are going?"

He glanced at her, but there was no surprise in his expression. He had known she wasn't sleeping. "I must."

Gathering the sheet to her breasts, she sat up, feeling a coldness wash over her. "You are going to fight."

He frowned. "You will be safe here."

"You will not be safe, though," she said shakily. "You were going off to war without saying anything to me at all?"

He grimaced. "I would rather take the memory of the sweetness of our time together with me for warmth than the bitter taste of yet another argument. Do not demand something of me that I can not give you."

Chapter Twenty

Aliya felt a welling of hurt that almost took her breath. Her mind instantly interpreted that to mean he could not profess feelings for her that he did not have. She could not be certain that that was what he meant, of course. It occurred to her that he might be referring to her demand that he try to make peace with her father, but she knew well enough that that opportunity had passed. No one spoke directly to her about the things that were happening beyond the walls of Tetan and beyond the borders of Goldone, but she had heard enough to know that no one would be untouched by the war that had broken out.

She found, though, that she really didn't want to know what he had meant. When he was safe and had returned, that would be soon enough to speak of what they felt for one another, to draw the boundaries between them if there were to be any.

She didn't want to think that he might be distracted by anything she had said, particularly an argument, when he needed his full attention on the business of staying alive. "I only wanted to ask that you take care of yourself ... for me."

He studied her for a long moment and finally moved back to the edge of the bed. Leaning down, he kissed her with a heat that belied their recent satiation with one another. To her disappointment, though, he did not linger.

When he reached the door, he paused and turned, surveying the room. "I had not realized before what was missing from my home."

Aliya sent him a questioning look, wondering what particular thing she had done that had pleased him. The bed hangings perhaps? The rug she had spread on the floor between the bed and the hearth? "What?"

He smiled faintly, his gaze caressing her. "You."

An unidentifiable emotion constricted her chest at that, squeezing her heart.

"I will return in a few days. You must be ready then to travel light and fast, for I will most likely move my household."

Aliya was so stunned by that announcement that she was still staring at him in disbelief when he exited the room. Was it as bad as that, she wondered fearfully?

She had been certain that the royal palace was virtually impregnable. That had given her no comfort, at first, when she had only thought in terms of being freed by her father. When she had realized that her feelings had changed completely and that she was content to stay with Talin, even if she was not completely content to hold only the place of his second wife, she had looked upon the situation of the palace with relief. Whether her father would talk peace or not seemed to matter little so long as he could not actually engage in war with the folk of Tetan.

She should have known the moment she realized that Talin was planning to go out and meet the army that something had changed the whole face of the war.

And there could be only one reason that Talin had begun to doubt the invincibility of his fortress in the sky.

Her father had brought in a conjurer of the black arts.

She should have known that, she realized, when she had seen what had happened to Solly. Instead, she had been so completely wrapped up in her personal concerns that she had not considered how alarmed Talin had been about it, indeed all of the castle folk.

It chafed her to think she could do nothing but wait and worry. As hard as she worked to fill her days with worthwhile tasks that kept her from feeling completely useless, her mind still wavered back and forth between wondering where Talin was and how he was faring and trying to figure some way that she could reach out to her father and try to stop the madness before the land ran red with the blood of innocents.

It was a waste of time, of course. There was no way that she could leave the palace unless she could convince someone to take her, and she not only doubted she could convince anyone to do what would amount to treason, but she could not bring herself even to try. If she had been more certain that she could reason with her father, she might have felt that the risk was not too much to ask, but she was not at all certain he would even speak to her, let alone listen. And she did not think she wanted anyone else's blood on her hands.

The penalty for treason was death, a slower death, perhaps, in peace time, a swift one in times of war.

* * * *

Of all the clans of the man beast, the Wyvern were the only folk who had focused their beast inward and discarded what they had considered the dubious advantage of their ability to change form. Since they no longer had the gift of flight, it fell to the other clans who still had that gift--the Golden Falcon, the Condor, and the Eagle--to handle the bombardment of the army formed up on the plains below them.

The clan of the Condor, led by Hadrian, attacked first, but either because they had less bravery, or less experience, their bombardment was largely ineffectual, for they did not fly low enough before releasing to hit a great deal.

Talin contained his fury with an effort. Although it did not escape him, or anyone else for that matter, that the Condor managed to stay well out of range of the archers, he realized they would have to give them the benefit of doubt if they were not to part ways at once.

The clan of the Eagle did somewhat better. They, at least, displayed no hesitancy about flying low enough to do considerable damage, but their accuracy left something to be desired and many became so enraged when they saw how little actual damage they were doing that they ceased the bombardment and began diving at the soldiers below, slashing at them with their rapier sharp talons and beaks until the soldiers finally drove them off or killed them.

His own clansmen, either from an equal but opposing idiocy, or from a misplaced determination to make quick work of a bad business, took chances they should not have. Their bombardment was effective, more than any had anticipated, for they flew so low to drop their bombs that he lost damned near a quarter of his men to the archers, who felt smug right up until the moment that the great Falcons began to rain from the sky. The deaths of the man beasts brought about utter chaos as they slammed into the earth, killing or maiming any of the man children unfortunate enough to be standing in their path and too slow to get out of the way.

It turned the tide of the battle, however. The ranks broke and the panicked men began to run. Before the leaders could rally their men and return the ranks to order, the army of the man beasts, many of them armored as the man children were, charged from the forest surrounding the battlefield, cutting down hundreds of the man children before they even realized that they had fled right into an ambush.

By the time the sun began to set, the bodies of the man beasts and the man children littered the ground for miles. Both armies withdrew to count their losses and lick their wounds.

In consideration of those among his men who were too wounded to withdraw any great distance, which included Talin himself, the Falcon clan settled in the foothills to do what they could for the wounded. The Wyvern had brought with them potions concocted by the Wizard Mortiver, but these, they found, were largely ineffectual against the magic the man children brought to battle. Those who had been 'bitten' by the poison tipped arrows died in spite of everything anyone could think to do. Those, like Talin, who had been fortunate enough only to catch the shafts with invisible tips survived because Talin had learned that only removing what they could see would not be enough. Weakened by the loss of blood, they had, perforce, to remain where they were for another full day before they were all strong enough to move on.

There was some sense of accomplishment to buoy their spirits. Despite their own losses, which were great, they had managed to do what they had set out to. They had whittled the man children's army down to a size they had some chance of defeating.

Certain King Andor would gather what remained of his army and move as quickly as he could now to join with the army from across the sea, Talin took his own clan members home to rest and recuperate while they could.

Despite the dangerous amount of time Talin had allowed for the injured to heal, he was so weak and exhausted by the time he reached the palace that he was aware of very little beyond the fact that Aliya had come out to watch their return. When he woke later, he discovered that he was ensconced in his bed and Aliya sat near the hearth as she had before when he had been injured.

This time he had not had to feign being worse off than he was. He did not even have a clear memory of the trip from the foothills home.

As if she sensed his gaze, Aliya looked up from the needle she was plying. Smiling when she saw he was awake, she set her needlework aside and crossed the room, settling one hip on the edge of the bed. "Hungry?"

The warmth he'd felt at her nearness vanished. "If it is to be gruel, then no."

Aliya chuckled. "I will send for whatever you like."

Catching her around the waist, he dragged her across his body and pressed her into the mattress. "I hunger for you," he murmured, burrowing his face against her throat.

"I am not at all certain that is the sort of sustenance you need right now," she murmured.

"Which goes to show you have no notion of what I need."

She stroked his hair and ran a hand lightly along his back. As tempting as it was to give in to his lovemaking, she did not want to tire him more and delay his recovery. In any case, there were matters of state that required his attention. "There is someone waiting to see you."

Talin lifted his head to look at her quizzically.

"The council elders returned while you were gone. They have brought a man whom they believe will be able to help us."

Talin's gaze sharpened, flicking over her face measuringly. Somehow, she didn't think that was entirely because of her announcement, but instead of pursuing the matter, she climbed off of the bed and moved to the bell pull she had had installed, glancing back to see if Talin was suitably impressed.

He was watching her curiously.

When a maid appeared after a few moments and she sent the woman to fetch the visitor, he frowned. "As much as I enjoy your coddling, I am not so weak and ill that I must receive in my bed," he said chidingly.

"But you will indulge me?"

He sent her a wicked glance. "Only because it suits my own preferences at the moment," he murmured in a voice laden with promise.

As tempting as it was to pursue that line of conversation, Aliya knew the elders had been waiting impatiently to be allowed to speak to Talin so she merely sent him an arch look and crossed the room to retrieve her work basket.

"Stay," Talin said when he saw her intent.

Aliya glanced at him in surprise. "They might not be comfortable speaking of state matters in front of me," she pointed out.

"They will get over it."

Shrugging, Aliya settled with her work once more. A few moments later, there was a tap at the door. At Talin's summons, the council members trooped in followed by a fifth man.

Talin pushed himself slowly upright as he studied the stranger.

His attire was strange enough, for he wore only a length of pure white fabric wrapped around his waste that ended at his knees and resembled a very short skirt rather than breeches or loincloth. His strange appearance went far beyond that, however, for his skin was golden, more like the precious metal than his own tan skin, which was more of a warm brown than real gold.

The hair that grew from his head and fluttered around his shoulders in a long, straight mass was cerulean.

"I am Syrian," the man said, bowing respectfully. "I am most happy to offer my services to your cause."

Talin frowned. "You are a wizard?"

Syrian smiled apologetically. "Alas, no. I am well versed, however, in Alchemy, which you may find useful. Primarily, I have come to offer my gift of sight."

Talin glanced from the man to the council elders, who were beaming at him as if they had produced a miracle. "My own sight is quite keen," he said slowly, wondering if he would have to guess what purpose the elders had thought the man would serve.

Syrian's smile broadened. "Apologies that I failed to make myself clear, Sire. But even you can not see what I can see."

"What is it that you can see?"

"The future. The past. What will be. What might come to pass. I am a Seer."

Talin merely stared at the man for many moments. Finally, he nodded. "I am not interested in hearing how the war will end," he said finally, keeping the irritation from his voice with an obvious effort.

Looking unperturbed, the Seer merely bowed. "Would you find it useful to know where your army will go? When? How many men he will have with him? What strategy he has planned for each confrontation? Would you find it helpful to know what magic he uses so that you would know how to guard yourself against it?"

Talin looked at him with more interest. "You can see these things?"

Syrian nodded. "I will not boast that I can always see all things, but many things, yes, that will help you in this battle with your enemy."

Talin frowned. "What could I offer you in return that you could not gain for yourself?"

"Acceptance. A home. Peace among people who will not despise me for being different."

Talin considered it for several moments and finally shook his head. "I can not guarantee any of that save that I will do what I can for you if you will help me to save my people. I will see to it that you find a place among the man beasts, respect, and peace from harm or pursuit. But only you can ensure your acceptance."

Syrian executed a movement that was somewhere between a salute, a bow, and a nod. "I do not expect to receive what is not yours to give," he murmured and then glanced at Aliya, his expression growing somber, his eyes sad. "And I can not prevent a war that was foretold long ago." He returned his attention to Talin. "I am here because it was written that I would be the instrument of the man beasts' salvation. When the elders came, I knew that it was time."

* * * *

"I know you are afraid, Aliya," Talin said gently. "But I will not allow harm to come to you. Do not argue with me on this."

Aliya frowned. "I can not believe that I would be safer elsewhere than I am here. The palace can not be scaled by the army you are facing. The spire which holds it aloft in the sky is higher than any tree. How could they climb up even to begin an assault? They can not fly as you can."

Talin's face hardened. "They have magic, Aliya. They do not need to come up. I can not be certain that their magic would not bring it down, and if that happened you could not escape on your own--nor your ladies."

Aliya felt something cold clench inside of her at the image that instantly brought into her mind. She nodded.

Talin pulled her close, his arms tightening around her. "I do not like this any more than you do. There is safety in the place we have found, but little comfort."

Aliya smiled against his chest. "I am not so fragile as you seem to believe. I can handle the discomfort and will, gladly, if it eases your mind." She hesitated for a moment. "It is the flight there that petrifies me."

"Shameful," Talin murmured with a chuckle. "You are the concubine of the king of the Golden Falcon! You should not quake only at the thought of flying."

She pulled away and looked up at him but she found it difficult to smile.

Kissing her lightly on the forehead, he released her. "You are packed?"

She nodded, moving to the bed and lifting the strap to show him that the pack he had given her was full. He grasped the strap and tugged, pretending it was too heavy to lift and drawing a rueful smile.

"It is not that full!" she said with a chuckle.

He tapped her chin and then flicked a finger along her cheek. "That is better.

It was dark when they reached the courtyard. The moon had set long since and dark clouds skidded across the sky, obscuring even much of the stars. Aliya shivered, turning to glance at Lady Beatrice and Lady Leesa who were huddled together in fright nearby.

When she turned to look at Talin again, he stood before her as a great falcon. "This time I will carry you on my back. It will more comfortable for you, I think."

"It could not be less," Aliya quipped, wondering how she was supposed to climb up on his back and if she could hang on tightly enough to keep from falling. Someone touched her arm and she turned to see that Solly had come up beside her. Bowing, he grasped her around the waist and lifted her up. When she was settled against his soft, warm feathers, he handed her the satchel, which she slung across her shoulder. To her surprise, instead of walking away, he began to fiddle with some sort of leather harness, which he draped across Talin's back and then fastened beneath his belly. Lifting a strap, he moved one over each of her shoulders.

Relief flooded her.

She should have known that Talin would take care that she was safe!

The flight was unnerving for all that she felt reasonably secure and could not see the vast emptiness beneath her. Talin had told her to dress warmly, and she had, but she was still chilled to the bone and her teeth chattering by the time they at last began to descend again.

As relieved as she was to know that their journey was ending, a terrible sense of dread began to seep into her, for she knew that Talin would leave her here, and she was not at all certain that she would see him again.

Chapter Twenty One

The place they were going, Talin had told Aliya once they were airborne, had once been a part of the temple built on Mount Carceras to the old gods. The temple had been erected on top of the caverns that, it had once been said, led to the underworld and the realm of the demons, so that the old gods could guard the gateway and prevent the evil ones from escaping into the world of man.

Aliya wasn't certain of whether to believe him or not, for she was more than half inclined to think he had only mentioned the underworld to unnerve her. "But it isn't … is it?"

Talin had chuckled. "No, love. It is only a labyrinth of caves, but they are deep in the earth and will offer protection from most anything. And since they lie in the land of Memnon and the dragon clan dwells there no longer, few even know of them."

It was obvious that effort had been put forth, even in such trying times, to make the caverns as comfortable for those who would be seeking shelter there as possible, but it would have taken a good deal more to make the place truly comfortable. Aliya was too miserable emotionally to notice the discomfort at first, but after two nights of sleeping on a pallet on the uneven floor of the cavern, physical discomfort began to take the upper hand.

Beyond the painful, scattered pebbles that were everywhere, biting into tender flesh sitting, lying, or standing, the cavern was damp and chilly. They did not dare light a very large fire or keep it going for very long. The smoke had a tendency to hang like a pall above them and once there, did not dissipate appreciably. Beyond the choking smoke, there was little wood and they had been cautioned not to go out unless the situation was dire.

They had food for at least a week, water, firewood, torches for light, bedding for pallets and each other for entertainment.

Aliya's ladies complained endlessly. By the second day, the other occupants of the cavern had begun to look at them as if they were contemplating shoving their heads beneath the water in the pool and holding them there until the water stopped bubbling.

Aliya felt the temptation herself.

"I do not see why it would hurt to go up only for a few moments to catch a breath of fresh air," Lady Leesa grumbled as they settled on their pallet for the third night. "Surely, it is dark outside and no one would be around to see us anyway."

"Go, if you want to," Aliya finally snapped irritably. "But if you are lost, you will have to find your own way back."

Leesa sniffed irritably. "We should all go."

"No," Aliya said firmly. "Talin brought us here because he was concerned for our safety. I am not going to jeopardize everyone's wellbeing only because I am uncomfortable. Soon, they will return for us. I am sure of it."

"I'll go with you," Lady Beatrice volunteered. "I think, perhaps, I could stand this a little better if I might have a few moments' respite."

"Just be quiet," Aliya warned them.

She settled when they'd left, trying not to worry that they might inadvertently give their hiding place away. Surely, she thought, if it was not dark, they would know better than to take a chance on going out?

She shook the thought off. They were sensible. That was one of the reasons her father had chosen them for her--the fact that they could be relied upon to keep a cool head and behave responsibly.

She was almost sorry she hadn't gone with them. There had been a coolness between them since they had argued about Talin and she had sent them to stay with the other maids. She supposed the coolness was mostly her fault and that they felt that they were in disfavor.

They had been for a while. She still did not want to listen to them speaking against Talin, but she did miss the closeness they had had between them before.

Maybe, if she made the effort to close the gap, they would also, and they would eventually come to see that Talin was a good man.

She dozed, awakening only a short time later as some grasped her arm.

"Princess!" Lady Beatrice said in a hissing whisper. "Lady Leesa has turned her ankle."

Drunk from sleep, Aliya struggled to rouse herself and make sense of the urgency in Beatrice's voice. "What?"

"We were walking in the ruins above, but we did not dare to take the torch and could not see. I think she has only twisted her ankle, but she is in pain and I don't think I can help her by myself."

Aliya threw her covers off and got to her feet unsteadily. Grasping her arm, Lady Beatrice led her quickly from the cavern and along the long, natural tunnel that climbed steeply toward the mountain top above them.

"I should have brought my medicines!" Aliya exclaimed in sudden irritation when they reached the stairs at the end of the tunnel that had been hewn from the rock to join the temple above them with the labyrinth of caves beneath.

"It will be best anyway to get her down here before you try to give her anything for the pain, else it might take more than the two of us to manage it."

Nodding, Aliya lifted her skirts and hurried up the stairs. They paused at the top so that Lady Beatrice could extinguish the torch. Blinded as they were plunged abruptly into abject darkness, Aliya place a hand along the wall and very carefully felt her way up the last few stairs and along a short passage through the base of a crumbling statue.

She had just stepped into the opening when Beatrice uttered a faint gasp and slammed against her so hard they both pitched forward, plowing into the ground. Stunned by the impact and the blow that had come directly before it, it was several moments before Aliya actually grasped that the hands pulling at her weren't the helping hands of someone trying to get her up, but the hands of someone binding her. "What are you doing?" she gasped in disbelief.

"You will thank us for this one day," Lady Leesa whispered shakily.

"Thank you?" Aliya demanded disbelievingly as the two women hauled her to her feet. "How dare you manhandle me like this! I am your princess!"

"It is because we love you," Lady Beatrice said briskly, shoving a cloth into Aliya's mouth and then securing it in place with a strip of linen.

She'd been too stunned with disbelief even to think of trying to flee from them or to struggle. By the time she came to her senses enough to realize the need, it was too late. Her hands were bound tightly behind her back and she could not even scream for help. "..itch!" she snarled. "Weh go!"

"Shhh!" Lady Leesa hissed. "They will hear you!"

"Ooo?"

Ignoring her, each grasped an arm and started hauling her away from the temple ruins. It was dark, and with little light from the sky to show them the way, they stumbled over rocks and brush, nearly falling time and again. After perhaps fifteen minutes, her ladies pulled her to a halt. "Look!" Lady Beatrice whispered in excitement, pulling Aliya around until she could see, far in the distance, campfires.

"It's your father's army! I know it. We are saved!"

She didn't want to be saved! She wanted to go back, but they had gagged her and she could do nothing more than make furious, unintelligible noises. Despite her struggles, they dragged her onward, finding a narrow track after a while that led down the side of the mountain to the valley below it where the army of Talin's enemies lay waiting.

Dread dogged her every step of the way. At first, her only thoughts were that Talin would think she had betrayed him and seized the first opportunity to escape him. After a while weariness began to set in and as it did, a new, even more dreadful fear began to take hold of her.

Lady Beatrice and Lady Leesa knew where the caverns were, the caverns where Talin had hidden the children, the women who were with child, and the ancients. Her weariness vanished at that thought and a coldness washed over her that seemed to make her mind work at frantic speed, searching for something she could do to prevent her father from finding them and slaughtering them.

She felt like weeping when nothing at all came to mind. She should have struggled harder, she raged inwardly. If she had, someone might have heard. They might have at least been alerted to danger. Instead, she had crept out of the cavern quietly to keep from waking anyone, fallen right into the trap her ladies had set for her without a clue of what was going on.

If she could only get them to take the gag from her mouth perhaps she could reason with them?

She began to fake coughing and gagging. The problem was, the moment she did, she began to cough and gag in earnest. Alarmed, Lady Leesa jerked the linen away from her mouth and snatched the wad of cloth out. Aliya sucked in a wheezing breath, coughing and choking at the dryness of her mouth until she had to struggle to keep from throwing up. Finally, the spasms passed.

"Better?" Lady Beatrice asked anxiously.

Aliya swallowed with an effort. "Thirsty."

"We did not bring any water. We did not bring anything at all," Lady Leesa said in a distressed voice. "We are not far from the camp, now, though. I am sure of it."

Lifting her head at the note of anxiety in Lady Leesa's voice, Aliya looked around. "I do not see the campfires," she said in surprise.

The three of them turned in a circle. "I do not see them either," Lady Beatrice exclaimed in alarm, and then looked up at the sky as if she would find answers there.

"The track we followed must have wound around a hill. Or perhaps it cut back?" Lady Leesa said worriedly.

"It does not matter," Lady Beatrice said decisively. "I am sure this is the right direction. We will find them. Or they will find us."

Aliya was just as certain that Lady Beatrice was wrong about the direction since she had watched as the campfires disappeared behind a rise in the land, but she kept that to herself. If they wandered around in the dark long enough neither woman would be able to say for certain where the women and children of the clan were hidden and, with any luck at all, her father would not spare the time to search. She prayed fervently that he wouldn't. Talin might never forgive her for what he saw as a betrayal of him, but she would never forgive herself if her stupidity led to the deaths of his people.

Their reception in her father's camp was worse than Aliya had anticipated. Aside from the fact that everyone they passed along the way to her father's tent eyed her either with contempt or thinly veiled speculation, her father received her with the coldness of a complete stranger.

"Sire!" Lady Beatrice exclaimed the moment they were escorted inside the tent, dropping into a deep curtsey. "We have rescued the princess!"

King Andor looked the three of them over as if someone had just upended a chamber pot at his feet, his gaze focusing for many long moments on the bindings.

"Welcome home, daughter," he finally said, his voice as cold as his icy pale eyes.

* * * *

To Aliya's vast relief, there was no search for the women of the clan. Despite the fact that she had wandered for many hours trying to make certain that Lady Leesa and Lady Beatrice were thoroughly lost, they had only to mention the temple and her father knew exactly where he could find them. Fate smiled upon them, however, for he was in too great a hurry to meet and join with the army he was marching toward to spare the time to slaughter them.

He would take care of that, he assured her, once the armies of man had destroyed the unnaturals and wiped them from the face of the earth forever.

It was for the same reason, so he said, that he could not spare the time to return her to her home himself, or men to take her.

She knew better. The truth was in his eyes. He meant to see to it that he killed them all and he wanted her to be there to see her lover die.

Lady Beatrice and Lady Leesa had fallen over themselves to explain why they had 'rescued' her and brought her back bound and gagged. It was because, they said, that she had been enthralled by the man beast, and could not break the spell, though they were certain King Andor's wizard could.

Perhaps they even believed that.

Her father did not and Aliya made no attempt to convince him that he was wrong.

She did not attempt to speak to him about making peace either, for he was not the man she had thought she had known and she saw that nothing she could say would sway him. She would have been willing to beg, to cry--to promise him anything he demanded, but she knew it was useless. There was nothing for her in his eyes, not regret, nor pity, no love, no understanding--just an emptiness, as if his soul had been sucked from his body and left only a husk with the fevered eyes of a fanatic.

She wondered if, perhaps, he had gone mad ... or she had.

* * * *

Aliya sat stiffly erect on the palfrey at her father's side, trying to close her mind to the horror she had been brought to witness. It was a formidable task, for the sights and sounds and smells of battle surrounded her in a noxious haze. It was barely daylight and already her father had lost a good portion of his army. The bombardment from above had begun to rain death upon the encampment before the soldiers were even fully awake. Everyone had scrambled into the nearness garment to hand, and run to gather horses and weapons, trying to create order out of the chaos of terror, to no avail. She and her father had been hurriedly mounted on horses half crazed with fear. One of the royal guards had snatched her reins from her hands and led her horse as they had charged out of the encampment and raced toward the hill her father had chosen as his watch post for the battle--which was not to have begun before first light.

By first light, the encampment was empty of the living. The soldiers had not marched to the field chosen for battle so much as they had stampeded in the general direction of it, driven there by their commanders, and there had been no let up since to give the captains the opportunity to bring any real order to the battle.

It was melee in the truest sense of the word, a mad, fear and hate driven rampage of hacking and slashing and firing wildly, only to have the chance to draw one more breath.

As terrified as Aliya was, a fierce gladness stole over her as she saw that the army of the man beasts had surprised the armies of her father and his allies, for even she could see that they were grossly outnumbered.

It took all she could do to keep from searching the sky for a glimpse of Talin. Fear kept her eyes staring blindly straight ahead. Her father was in a rage such as she had never seen before, cursing steadily beneath his breath when he was not screaming orders at his couriers, who had already plowed a path from the hillside to the battle field carrying orders back and forth at a frantic pace. He was enraged enough to have his careful plans routed before he could even implement them. He was already furious to have his 'tainted' daughter beside him as a constant reminder that Talin had humiliated him by snatching his greatest treasure from beneath his nose. She did not want to chance that he might think to use her to taunt Talin, to try to draw him to his death.

She had no idea how effective such a ruse might prove, or if Talin even knew that she was no longer in the caverns. But she did not want to chance it, regardless.

She could not tell an appreciable difference in the fear clawing at her belly, or the nausea, but after a time she began to be less aware of it and more aware of her discomfort. Her rump grew numb in the saddle. Her back and shoulders began to ache from holding herself stiffly erect for so long. Her skin began to feel as if the sun would burn her flesh off as it moved slowly across the sky.

The orb had nearly reached its zenith when the bombardment ceased almost as abruptly as it had begun. Before anyone could draw a breath of relief, the shrieks, cries and bellows issuing from hundreds of demon throats sent a new rash of fear crawling over their skin and the 'unholy' army of the man beasts appeared on the crest of the surrounding hills, charging down into the scattered, broken army of the man children.

The allied armies of man regrouped, forming a near solid mass in the center of the valley.

Aliya was nearly unseated as her reins were jerked and the entire party of which she was a part, raced from the hill along a downward sloping crest, then up another. Following the brow of the hills, they came at last upon one higher than the one they had occupied before, slightly more distant and there the kings took up watch again over their chess game.

Aliya flicked a glance at the stone faced warrior that held her reins. His gaze was as fixated upon the battle below them as everyone else's, but she could see he had the ends of her horse's reins wrapped around one fist. As casually as she could, she surveyed the men around her.

She discovered that she was positioned near the center.

Disappointment and frustration washed over her.

Even if she could somehow manage to snatch the reins away from the man who held them, she was still trapped.

With an effort, she forced herself to relax the tension in her shoulders, watching the men around her now rather than the battle below, hoping an opening would come. Slowly, the sun crawled across the sky and the tight little knot of men and horses eased as her father and his allies shifted positions to keep an eye on the fight as it turned in first one direction and then another.

Realizing after a while that the wild idea of snatching her reins free and fleeing was not going to happen, Aliya finally shifted in her saddle and prepared to dismount.

"Stay put," the man guarding her growled.

She gave him a cold look. "I have to relieve myself."

She might as well have shouted it, for every man on the hillside turned to look at her with varying degrees of suspicion. She glared them balefully. Finally, her father nodded at the man, jerking his chin toward an outcropping of rock.

Frustration rose in her again, but she did her best to contain it, to appear unconcerned as the guard helped her down from the horse and walked her to the back edge of the hill. "Stay where I can see you," he growled when he finally released her arm and allowed her to move beyond the view of the others.

Ignoring him, she moved a little further away, glancing at the outcropping of rock as if her only interest was in gaining privacy. When she glanced toward the guard again, she saw that he had closed the distance she was trying so hard to gain between them. "*Must* you watch me piss?" she demanded indignantly.

Instead of looking either startled or shamed, as she had hoped, he leered at her. "I must."

Grinding her teeth, she turned her back to him, adjusted her clothing and squatted, raking her eyes along the ground in search of a rock. She spied one of a manageable size not far from where she'd settled. It was still just beyond reaching it without attracting his attention, unfortunately. Fluffing her skirts, she shifted a little closer, hoping she wouldn't discover when she grasped the thing that it was not loose as she thought, but instead the protruding point of a larger rock.

Relief went through her when she grasped it. Rolling it beneath the edge of her skirts, she made a great business out of adjusting her clothing once more and gripped the rock as she rose, tucking it beneath a fold in her gown.

She didn't look at the guard, afraid that he would see her intent in her expression. Instead, she watched her steps as he grasped her arm and led her back to her palfrey. When he released her arm and encircled her waist to lift her onto the horse's back, she swung the rock at his head, planting it solidly along the side. As he released her and staggered back, she yanked her skirts to her knees and raced for the rocky hillside, stumbling and nearly falling, righting herself. Her heart was hammering so loudly in her chest and ears it deafened her to pursuit, but the man had let out a curse when she struck him. She knew even if surprise had slowed their reaction, they would be after her in moments.

A dark shadow closed over her, distracting her as she clambered over a rock. Glancing around, she saw three of the royal guards closing in on her rapidly. Gasping, she tried to run faster. The reckless speed cost her her footing. Stepping on a loose rock, she skidded, pin wheeled her arms trying to regain her balance and lost the battle, pitching forward. Pain shot through her hands, arms and shoulders as she caught herself. Before she could push herself upright again, a heavy weight landed on her legs.

Closing her hands around the mixture of loose soil and rocks beneath her palms, she twisted, pitching the debris at the man's face. In the sky above, she caught a glimpse of a great Golden Falcon. It was plummeting straight toward them and she knew instantly that it must be Talin.

Horror filled her as she realized that she had lured him by her own actions into just the trap she had feared her father would set. Wrestling frantically with the man that had managed to retain his grip on her in spite of the fact that she'd blinded him with the dirt, Aliya beat him on the head with her balled fist and finally began grabbing at rocks and pelting him with them. He lost his grip trying to shield his face from the rocks and she scrambled away.

She could see even as she managed to win free, though, that the other two guards had stopped the moment they thought their comrade had her. One had no weapon and had charged back toward the main group, but the other man had already placed a quiver in his cross bow and was cranking the string back frantically.

"No!" she screamed, whirling abruptly and charging back toward the man with the bow.

The guard she'd just hammered with rocks was halfway up when she raced past him. He made a grab for her and managed to grasp a handful of her skirts, jerking her to a halt before she could reach the one with bow. To her horror, she saw him taking aim. Without stopping to consider, she bent down, grabbed a rock and hurled it at the man.

The 'rock' wasn't a rock at all, but rather a hard clump of dirt and smaller rocks. It exploded as it hit the man's shoulder, startling him, spattering the side of his face and neck with tiny missiles. She screamed as his finger jerked the trigger and the bolt flew free, lifting her head to watch its path. Above them, she caught a glimpse of the falcon as he swerved abruptly.

Before she could be certain of whether or not he had managed to avoid the bolt, she found herself surrounded by men and horses. She was jerked up and tossed across her saddle on her belly, kicking and screaming as the entire party pelted down the hillside. The first jolt that went through her as her mount leapt into a gallop knocked the wind from her lungs. Before she could think to try to slide off, or fall from her precarious perch, someone leaned down, curled fingers into the back of her gown and jerked her from the bouncing back of the horse.

Even as she struggled to catch her breath, she swung wildly at the man who was trying to drag her onto the front of his saddle. He dragged her up in spite of her best efforts, finally grasping her hair painfully and pulling back on her head until she thought her neck would snap. Something cold and sharp dug into her throat, taking the fight out of her instantly.

Her gaze flew to the man's face, and then upwards in search of Talin.

He wheeled in a tight circle overhead and abruptly shot away, shrinking in a matter of moments to no more than a dot far up into the sky.

With an effort, she swallowed against the pressure on her throat, squeezing her eyes closed at the sting. She thought for several moments that the man would follow through with his threat and slice her throat. After an endless moment of time, though, the blade was slowly withdrawn.

Releasing his grip on her hair after a few moments, the man settled her more firmly in his lap, gripped her waist tightly with one hand and the pommel with the other.

One of the other guards had grabbed his reins when he dropped them to ward Talin off by threatening her.

Weak in the aftermath of her brief, if furious, struggle, shaky with relief that Talin had come so near dying in an attempt to rescue her, she leaned limply, if resentfully, against the man behind her, too weary to hold herself aloof even though it irked her that she could not.

The hostility of the men surrounding her was almost palpable. She didn't need to look at them to see how they felt about her attempt to escape and her frantic efforts to keep them from shooting Talin. She could feel it.

Frustration brought stinging tears to her eyes. She had bungled her only chance. They would not allow her another one.

Chapter Twenty Two

When darkness cloaked the land in a heavy black veil, the man of the armies of both sides began to melt into it, slipping away to lick their wounds, count the living still among them and search for a better position for another assault. There were no tents pitched, no fires lit.

Dawn heralded another endless day of fighting and killing and being killed. As the sun set on the second day, both armies had whittled upon each other until there were fewer men standing than lying in pools of blood.

Again, as darkness closed over the gory battlefield, both armies withdrew to regroup. By dawn of the third day, Aliya was so exhausted she hardly knew where she was any longer. She could not fathom how the men could continue to fight when they had scarcely had time to eat or close their eyes.

The whole world had changed when the sun rose, washing the death fields with golden light, glinting off of the blood that coated almost every inch of earth.

The third day did not begin with the screams and shouts of man and beast, with the clatter of steel against steel. The ragged remnants of the allied army of men simply stared blank faced, dull with fatigue, at their enemies across the field.

Aliya was only vaguely aware of the hushed conversation around her, and not aware at all of the gist of it. When her father sent her a glance of contempt and snatched a strip of white fabric from his saddle bag, she merely stared at it uncomprehendingly.

Attaching it to the end of one of the staffs of the standard bearers, he nodded at the man. Nodding in response, the man lifted the standard, walked his horse to the edge of the hillside where they stood and then rose up in his saddle, slowly waving the standard back and forth.

Curious, but still without real comprehension of what was taking place, Aliya gazed across the field to see who he was waving at. Across the valley, a white flag appeared on the other side, waving back. As if they had only been waiting for that signal, her father and his allies turned their tired horses, straightened their backs, and spurred their horses forward. The royal guards fell in behind them, carrying Aliya with them as they rode down the hill to the valley and began to pick their way across the sea of dead and dying.

Already the stench of death was rising from the heat of the morning sun. Swallowing with an effort, Aliya covered her mouth and nose with her hand, trying to keep the bile from rising in her throat, trying to focus on anything besides the bodies her horse was daintily picking a path through. Skittish, shying and jerking its head as it tried to pull free of the man who led it every few moments, its nostrils quivering and flesh flicking, the horse she was mounted on reflected her own revulsion at traversing the valley of the dead.

They halted near the center, forming a line and Aliya saw then that they had been met there by the leaders of the clans of the man beasts. Abruptly alert, she scanned the long line until her gaze lit on Talin, scanning his body searchingly for signs of wounds.

Briefly, their gazes met, but he looked away almost at once as her father nudged his horse slightly forward of the others. "We will fight no more," he said, his voice loud and strident in the near deafening silence that held them in its grip.

Some of the tension seemed to ease from every man in both groups as the high king of the man beasts, who had stepped forward as her father had, nodded. "We will withdraw," he said in a deep, rumbling voice.

"You will agree not to seek retribution?" King Andor demanded.

The dragon king surveyed the men facing him. "Nothing will bring back the dead," he growled ominously. "...On either side."

King Andor nodded after a moment. "We will withdraw to rest and meet again here to discuss the conditions of peace."

"Nay. We will not!" the dragon king contradicted him in a rumbling voice. "There will never be true peace between our peoples, only animosity and renewed attempts to war as soon as you have recovered. We have no wish to live among you, side by side with our enemies, the man children. We have decided to take our people and go north to the land of shadows to carve out new kingdoms for ourselves.

"Know this! No man child shall ever step foot across our boundaries again and live to tell of it."

Aliya stared at the dragon king in dismay and then glanced quickly at Talin.

He would not meet her gaze. His face was as if carved from stone.

He thought she'd betrayed him, she realized. It was just as she had feared, and he would not speak up for her believing that she had returned to her father. "Wait!" she gasped before she had time to reconsider it. "I will go with you."

She shrank back as all eyes turned to her.

"Your place is with your own people!" her father growled ominously.

"My place is with my husband! Talin! For mercy's sake, I did not betray you. Do not let them do this!"

He glanced at her then, and she saw his gaze was filled with pain, not hate, but with knowledge, as well, of the inevitability of it. Her heart clenched in her chest painfully. "Your father is right," he said after a prolonged moment. "You belong with your own kind."

Aliya felt her chin wobble. She fought it, fought the tears clogging her throat. He loved her. Everything he had done spoke of love. It didn't matter than he had never said the words. She *knew* it in her heart!

It did matter! She wanted to hear it, needed to.

"Then tell me you do not care for me and I will stay with these people whom I have come to despise! I will live with their hate if you do not want me anymore."

His face twisted with pain. He opened his mouth to speak and closed it again. Swallowing thickly, he shook his head fractionally. "It does not matter. The high king has spoken."

Aliya stared at him for a long moment and then glanced at the dragon king hopefully. He studied her face searchingly, glanced at Talin's stony expression and then looked at her once more.

If you were with child then your place would be with your husband.

Aliya felt her jaw sag as the words flowed through her mind. Instinctively, she cupped a hand over her belly. She saw when she turned to look at Talin again that his gaze had focused upon her hand, become intent. "My child needs his father!" she announced baldly.

The look her father bent upon her made her quiver inside.

The dragon king almost seemed to smile. "She carries the child of a man beast. She must go with us for I will not allow the child to grow up among his enemies."

King Andor glared at her, grinding his teeth. Abruptly, he jerked on the reins, turning his horse and kicking it into motion. Almost as if they had practiced the steps and performed on a parade field, his allies and the royal guard turned as one and followed him.

Aliya felt the pain in her heart ease as she heard them ride away. One by one, the kings of the man beast clans turned away, as well, until at last Talin and Aliya stood alone in the center of the field, gazing at one another. Stepping forward at last, Talin grasped the horse's halter and looked up at her. "You will not see him again," he said slowly.

A spurt of pain clutched at her chest, but Aliya nodded. "He was lost to me long before now. Mayhap, in time, he will cease to hate me and think fondly of the daughter he once claimed to cherish--mayhap not. It does not matter. I belong with the man I love."

A faint smile curled his lips upward. Moving closer, he caught the pommel and swung himself up onto the horse behind her, wrapping his arms around her. "You are certain you will not come to regret being the devil's concubine?" he murmured, dipping his head to lavish a row of light kisses along the side of her throat.

"Not if that devil is you," she said huskily.

His arms tightened around her briefly. Finally, settling one along her waist to steady her, he took the reins and kicked the horse into motion. Aliya relaxed back against him as they finally left the battlefield behind. "You did not tell me you loved me," she said pensively.

He leaned down and nipped her earlobe with his teeth. "Did I not?" he asked teasingly.

She elbowed him in the ribs. "You know very well you have not said it."

"I adore you," he murmured, amusement threading his voice.

She let out an irritated huff of breath and he drew back on the reins, bringing the palfrey to a halt. Catching her chin, he tipped her face up and kissed her hungrily. "I love you," he murmured when he broke the kiss.

Aliya gazed up at him searchingly and was satisfied. "You will not be angry with me then?"

His brows rose questioningly.

"I am not with child," she admitted guiltily.

Talin chuckled, his arms tightening around her. "Do you think one man beast among us believed that for a moment?"

"No?" she asked, surprised and more than a little uneasy.

"No--especially not Balian, for he is no mere beast with the senses to know these things instinctively as is the case with the rest of us. He has powers far beyond any other."

Aliya smiled, feeling totally relaxed for the first time since she had lied, feeling warmth and gladness replace the anxiety that had been riding her. She had been accepted, welcomed by the king of kings.

"We must try to remedy that situation with all haste, however," Talin said huskily, spurring the palfrey once more.

The End

Return to a realm of fantasy and forbidden love in The Shadowmere Trilogy, now available in Trade Paperback wherever books are sold.

The Shadowmere Trilogy by Jaide Fox: Trade Paperback
ISBN 1-58608-670-7

In a land shrouded in darkness, protected by magic and the fierceness of its people--for those who venture into these forbidden lands, the penalty is death ... or worse. But sometimes it is not the monsters who are to be feared, but the emptiness of an existence without love. For the first time, bring home the trilogy and discover passion and magic ... and love.

Untamed: When Lord Conrad captured a beastman as a sacrifice to heal her curse, Ashanti vowed to free the innocent man at any cost. Never did she expect her untamed captive would soon become her master....

Seduced by Darkness: Raphael, Lord of the Hunters, took Swan at the borderlands--mysterious, tempting ... and perilous to her very soul. For to give in to his dark seduction would be to consummate the sorcerer's curse ... and leave her forever the swan maiden ... and his prey.

The Dragon King: If Shadowmere had a ruler, Balian would be king. He is the most powerful of their number, feared above all others. And the time has come to find his mate.

Don't miss out on collecting these other exciting
Harmony™ titles for your collection:

Clone Wars: Armageddon by Kaitlyn O'Connor (Futuristic
Romance) Trade Paper 1-58608-775-4
*Living in a world devastated by one disaster after another,
it's natural for people to look for a target to blame for their
woes, and Lena thinks little of it when new rumors begin to
circulate about a government conspiracy. She soon
discovers, though, that the government may or may not be
conspiring against its citizens, but someone certainly is.
Morris, her adoptive father, isn't Morris anymore, and the
mirror image of herself that comes to kill her most
definitely isn't a long lost identical twin.*

Zhang Dynasty: Seduction of the Phoenix by Michelle M.
Pillow (Futuristic Romance) Trade Paper 1-58608-777-0
*A prince raised in honor and tradition, a woman raised
with nothing at all. She wants to steal their most sacred
treasure. He'll do anything to protect it, even if it means
marrying a thief.*

Warriors of the Darkness by Mandy M. Roth (Paranormal
Romance) Trade Paper 1-58608-778-9
*In place where time and space have no boundaries, ancient
enemies would like nothing more than to eradicate them
both, just when they've found each other.*

Printed in the United States
49360LVS00005B/82-99